GANGS OF SOCIAL MEDIA

VASIMRAJA **B**HAVIKATTI

Leadstart
INKSTATE

ISBN 978-93-90040-79-7

First published in India 2021 by Leadstart Inkstate
A Division of One Point Six Technologies Pvt Ltd

Sales Office:
Unit No.25/26, Building No.A/1,
Near Wadala RTO,
Wadala (East), Mumbai – 400037 India
Phone: +91 969933000
Email: info@leadstartcorp.com
www.leadstartcorp.com

Disclaimer: The views expressed in this book are those of the Author and do not pertain to be held by the Publisher.

Editor: Vaibhav Pathare
Cover: Nitin Ingale
Layouts: Kshitij Dhawale

Acknowledgements

I want to thank and express my sincere gratitude towards Ph.D. Scholars, graduate and undergraduate students of WhatsApp University. Their voluntary and involuntary, mindless, senseless message forwarding service has inspired this book. My sincere regards to the faculty members and especially to the Principal of WhatsApp University for creating such mindboggling fake content. Millions of misguided youth are on the path of enlightenment because of WhatsApp University. I am sure with your dedicated effort you will achieve the goal of eradicating the epidemic called 'common sense'.

Thank you once again.

About the Author

Vasimraja was born on 29th February 1984, in India. He currently lives in San Francisco Bay Area, California USA. He started reading fiction novels at the age of eight after overhearing a story narration of Sherlock Holmes by his father. He grew up in different towns of Northern Karnataka State before his family relocated to Dharwad, the literature capital of Karnataka where he met celebrated playwright and author, Late Girish Karnad. He was greatly influenced by Karnad's writing and personality.

Vasimraja works in the field of semiconductor engineering and has two patents on semiconductor memories. He is an avid reader of English, Kannada and Hindi literature. He presents the most complex ideas in a very simple form, leaving a lasting impression on readers.

Chapter 1

THE USUAL MORNING

It is 8 am, nice sunny morning in Bangalore, India. A young man in his late twenties dressed in casual blue trouser, a fine cotton white shirt with blue crisscross strips and Reebok running shoes is waiting for his office cab to arrive. The shoes are completely out of the match with his clothes. He checks the time on his watch and looks towards the street on his right. Still, there is no sign of his office cab. He has a good smartphone costing about Rs.25000 which he has bought a month ago. He has an engineering degree in Computer Science and works for a reputed software company as Senior Software Engineer.

In his office, he is known for his judgment and reasoning. He is the no-nonsense guy who does not take anything at face value. He reasons and questions everything. In his personal life, he is known to be a very friendly, jovial and credible person. But when it comes to his favorite pass time of forwarding messages in WhatsApp, all the characteristics which define him will be null and void. He just turns off his brain, he does not reason, nor doubt or question anything. The only thing which drives him during his pastime activity is blind emotion.

He is a member of several WhatsApp groups. He has one college group named as 'Backbenchers', one school group named as 'School days', office lunch group named as 'Lunch-party', family group which includes all his extended family members named as 'Parivar (Family)', he has one more college group named 'Strictly Boyz', which has only boys in the group and the list goes on.

Every day for about an hour especially during his office commute, the only thing he does is to forward messages from one group to another group. These are good morning messages, birthday wishes, jokes, political hoax, historical hoax, adult jokes, missing person information, patriotic messages, feel-good messages and on and on. Even though these are all different messages and coming in different groups, there are two things common about these messages. First, almost all the messages are forwarded. Second, most of these messages are not useful to the person who is receiving them. The only intent of these messages is to be forwarded, not to be read or understood. And yes, this young bright man also does the same thing for the next one hour, forward the messages.

This well-educated young man who practices reasonable judgment and logic in every aspect of his life is least bothered about authenticity, credibility or usefulness of WhatsApp messages before forwarding them.

He does this message forwarding voluntary service without giving a second thought because he has nothing to lose even if the message is false or a hoax. Nobody is going to judge him on the authenticity of his forwarded messages. He is not accountable for any messages he is forwarding. It does not damage his reputation, he does not lose money, it makes no difference to his friends and family if the message forwarded is a hoax. He loses his one hour of time but anyway he does not consider this one hour of commute to be of any productive use.

And today also he had planned to do the same.

He has about sixty-seven unread messages in his different WhatsApp group which are ready to be forwarded. But today, his favorite pass time of forwarding messages is going to cost him very heavily in a manner which he could not even imagine.

Meanwhile, at the same time, around 8 am, 2100 kilometers up north from Bangalore in New Delhi, another young man in his early thirties is about to board his Metro train and start his commute to the office which takes about forty-five minutes. He has a master's degree in business management and works for a very reputed financial firm. He is known for his street smartness. Carrying his laptop bag on his left shoulder, wearing an oversized, long sleeve, V-neck t-shirt, and blue denim jeans, he looks harmless. The glasses on his face almost take up the entire area of his cheeks and nose.

He is very similar to the person in Bangalore. He also has a good smartphone, rather a high-end one. He also does the same thing of forwarding the messages from one WhatsApp group to another WhatsApp group. He has one hundred and forty-four messages in his WhatsApp from several groups like College group, school group, office group, family group, etc.

In addition to these groups, he has one more specific group of a political party's cyber cell, it is named as Cyber Soldier. He is a very active member of this political party. Unlike the person in Bangalore, he doesn't stop at WhatsApp. He is active on Facebook and Twitter as well. Unlike the person in Bangalore who is driven by blind emotion while forwarding messages. This person in Delhi is driven by blind honesty and commitment to his political party.

His forwarded messages are clearly politically motivated. These messages include some historical messages which sound like a fact but often are myths. Some riots video which claims to happen in some remote village and mainstream media is refusing to cover it on purpose. Some anti-religious messages, some patriotic messages and so on. As an active member of a political party's cyber cell, he has one and only one job. To forward the messages from his Cyber Soldier group to all other groups. Leave alone authenticity or credibility, he does not even bother to read them. He just forwards them. That's it.

He goes one step forward with Facebook and Twitter. With Facebook, he must share, like or make a generic comment on whatever is published on his political party's page or any other pages related to his political party. There is no need to read, just share and spread the word, he does not care if the information is truth or hoax.

Same thing with Twitter, just keep re-tweeting the message from a political party or political leader. He doesn't care if the messages are true or hoax because he is not accountable for anything. He does not lose anything. But today he is going to pay a very heavy price for his carelessness.

In recent years, access to cheap and free internet gave rise to many kinds of social media trolls, most of these trolls are college students or unemployed youth who do it for pocket money. They get paid somewhere between Rs.30 (nearly 50 cents) to Rs.200 (nearly $2.50) for trolling on twitter, like this person who is located about 1000kms west of Bangalore in the city of Mumbai. Before he got into social media trolling, he ran a small business of desktop publishing and proofreading. Today being a paid social media troll, he neither cares for proof nor for reading.

Social media trolling is his secret business, which he operates from his same old office of desktop publishing which is nothing but a small cramped place below the staircase of a house, the place is so small where hardly anyone can stand or sit in comfort.

In this small place, the person has managed to fit in an office desk which has three computer screens probably connected to the same computer, a printer and a chair. He has multiple smartphones of different brands scattered around these computer screens.

In real life, he is a very well-mannered decent man. No one has ever heard a curse word from him, even when he is angry, he maintains his manners. But as social media troll, he can get as abusive as it can get. He can demean and insult anyone or anything to any extent. He has no moral boundaries of any kind.

He recently trolled a very famous celebrity actor for saying that he does not feel safe in Mumbai city as North Indians or Hindi speaking population in Mumbai are getting targeted. He used all the curse words to belittle the actor using a fake profile. He made another fake profile and made a decent but very vicious comment on twitter. He made another fake profile and replied to his comment posing as a supporter of the actor. He uses different ways to engage, provoke or distract attention. He is up for his next assignment today. He thought it will be business as usual. But very little did he know that he will be hit the hardest today and he will pay a very heavy price for his trolling.

These three in Bangalore, New Delhi and Mumbai widely represent the majority of the social media users in India.

Everyone is guilty of forwarding and sharing unverified messages without thinking of consequences. Some are driven by blind emotion, some are politically motivated, some are paid, some do it for fun. These include men, women, young, old, urban, rural, married, single, highly educated, uneducated, self-employed, professionals, rich, poor, middle class, celebrities, politicians, business leaders, you name it. Everyone willingly or unwillingly has become members of this gang.

You just need to have a smartphone, internet, and a social media account. That's it. Welcome to the gangs of social media, where there are no moral boundaries, no ethics, no common sense, no credibility, no authenticity, no difference between opinion and fact. Welcome to gangs of social media where everyone is an expert of everything, where there are no falsehoods but only alternative facts, where you can deny every reality that exists and create your version. With one tweet you can be a patriot and with another forwarded message, you can be anti-national. With one Facebook post you can be communal with another re-tweet you can be secular. No matter what you say, there are no consequences of any kind. But today it is all going to change.

Chapter 2

The Disruption

It is fifteen minutes past eight. The person in Bangalore is already seated in his cab and has started commute towards his office. He is the second pick up in this route. The lady from the previous pick up point is seated at the rear. He prefers to sit next to the driver. There is one more last pick up and off they go directly to the office. He greets the lady seated at the rear and smiles at the driver. He is very happy to see him wearing a seat belt, without being reminded. Finally, three months of daily intervention has yielded results, he thinks.

"Yen special evathu, surya bere dikhinida bandiro aagide…seat belt hakkundidera" he asked the driver in Kannada, which is the language spoken in Bangalore along with many other languages and which means

"What is special today, has the sun risen from the west, that you are wearing a seat belt"

"Yen ella saar, mama nithidane anthe next signal nalli" the driver replies in Kannada which means

"Nothing Sir, father-in-law is waiting in next signal," referring to the traffic cop as the father-in-law.

"Thuu nimma!!!, nimma mathe passenger safety gagi seat belt

hakondidera antha kushi aagithallrii."   He replied in Kannada, which means

"Damn you!!!, I was happy thinking that you wore a seat belt for your and passenger's safety." He replied with disappointment on his face.

He quickly settles after this brief exchange of words with the driver, wears his seat belt and rubs his palms on his thighs and gets ready for the action. Forwarding messages in WhatsApp for the next forty minutes to an hour.

The first message he sees is from his school group. It's a joke which reads.

> ➤ *Forwarded*
>
> Que: What is the difference between first bench students and last bench students?
>
> Ans: The first bench students don't forget teachers and teachers don't forget last bench students.

The joke brings a smile on his face and he forwards this message to his college group and family group.

In his family group, he sees his next message. The message is a picture, that shows different Maggi noodles packet and a test tube filled with blood marked as HIV+ . The picture claims that all Maggi products have HIV+ blood in it and it should be banned.

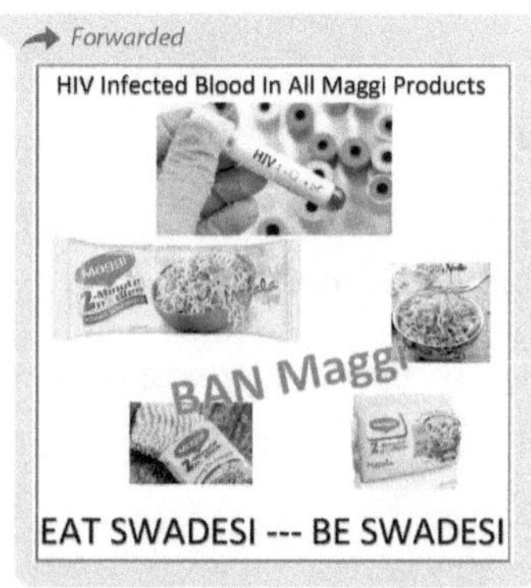

The person from Bangalore who is well educated and works for a reputed MNC without giving a second thought forwards this message to his school group and college group.

After the message is forwarded, he is about to look at other messages, but there is no movement on his phone. He keeps moving his fingers on the touch screen for a few seconds, but nothing happens. Thinking that WhatsApp is hung, he tries to navigate to other apps using the button at the bottom right of the phone, but nothing happens. He now looks concerned thinking that the phone itself is hung.

This is very unusual for the phone of this brand given that it is only a month old. He tries to switch off the phone holding its power button on top of the phone, but all efforts go in vain. He is now getting irritated and concerned. As he is getting ready to take out the phone's battery to give the phone a hard restart, the phone screen blinks and flickers for a few seconds. The flickering suddenly increases, and he is not able to see anything on the phone screen.

After a few more seconds of heavy flickering, it stops at once and a red screen is displayed on the phone. After a few seconds, a message in white bold font and all in capitals scrolls up, the message reads.

"YOU FORWARDED AN UNVERIFIED FALSE MESSAGE. YOU DIDN'T BOTHER TO CHECK IF MESSAGE WAS TRUE OR FALSE BECAUSE IT DOES NOT COST YOU ANYTHING. BUT TODAY YOU ARE GOING TO PAY,"

The message stays on the phone screen for about twenty seconds. Then another message starts scrolling

"YOUR PHONE WILL BE DESTROYED IN 12 HOURS ALL

YOUR PRIVATE INFORMATION INCLUDING PICTURES AND VIDEOS IN THIS PHONE WILL BE MADE PUBLIC,"

The message stays on the phone screen for about twenty seconds and then another message starts scrolling

"IF YOU WANT TO STOP THIS PAY Rs.1,00,000 ACC NO 007511156375890 CRYPTO CODE: SSWIB0045617,"

The message stays on the screen for a while, and the countdown begins

11:59:59… 11:59:58… 11:59:57… and it continues

He thinks it is a prank and all this time he is trying to restart his phone by holding the power button. He keeps trying to restart his phone, does all he can for the next five minutes to get his phone to work. After five minutes the message scrolls again

"YOU FORWARDED AN UNVERIFIED FALSE MESSAGE. YOU DIDN'T BOTHER TO CHECK IF MESSAGE WAS TRUE OR FALSE BECAUSE IT DOES NOT COST YOU ANYTHING. BUT TODAY YOU ARE GOING TO PAY"

The message stays on the phone screen for about twenty seconds. Then another message starts scrolling

"YOUR PHONE WILL BE DESTROYED IN 12 HOURS ALL YOUR PRIVATE INFORMATION INCLUDING PICTURES, VIDEOS, EMAILS AND MESSAGES IN THIS PHONE WILL BE MADE PUBLIC"

The message stays on the phone screen for about twenty seconds and then another message starts scrolling

"IF YOU WANT TO STOP THIS PAY Rs.1,00,000 ACC NO

007511156375890 CRYPTO CODE: SSWIB0045617" The message stays on the screen for a while, and the countdown continues

11:54:59… 11:54:58… 11:54:57… and it continues

He is totally confused and not able to understand what is happening. He is just holding his phone in his hands and staring at the phone screen. He now decides to give the phone a hard restart by taking off the battery of the phone. He quickly turns the phone upside down and removes the battery. The phone turns off, there is nothing on the screen. He keeps the battery and the back cover of the phone between his legs and holds the phone in his hand. He is still unclear about what has happened. After about a minute or two he inserts the battery back in the phone. He turns the phone around without closing the phone with the back cover. He now turns on the phone in the hope that it will be back to normal. The phone turns on at once and the message scrolls again.

"IF YOU WANT TO STOP THIS PAY Rs.1,00,000 ACC NO 007511156375890 CRYPTO CODE: SSWIB0045617"

The message stays on the screen for a while, and the countdown begins again

11:44:59… 11:44:58… 11:44:57… and it continues

He now realizes that something is wrong with the phone and probably it is infected by a virus. He is still in shock and complete disbelief about what has happened. He restarts his phone multiple times in the hope to revive it, but the same message keeps appearing with the time in the countdown decreasing. He removes the battery, sim card, and memory card multiple times and re-inserts but there is no sign of his phone coming back to normal. The same message keeps appearing that he forwarded an unverified false message and he must pay Rs.1,00,000 else his phone will be destroyed and all information on his phone will be made public. He is angry and frustrated.

Forty minutes have already passed, he hasn't realized that his co-passenger is already been picked up and is seated in the rear seat reading the newspaper. The lady who was already seated in the rear seat on the other side is taking a quick nap as she does daily. He hasn't realized that traffic is normal today, and the cab is about to reach the office in another five minutes. He hasn't realized that the driver has removed his seat belt after he has passed the traffic cop. All he knows that he is screwed because he forwarded an unverified false message.

He has now recollected his senses and realizes that he is in trouble. He is trying to recall who had forwarded this message to him. He doesn't remember. Until this moment he has never even bothered to pay attention to see who is forwarding him all these messages.

"Relatives are the most jealous and envious people in this world. They can never tolerate anyone's success apart from themselves." He says to himself as he recalls that the message was in the family group.

"One of my useless cousins, who are good for nothing must have done this to me." He says to himself clenching his teeth in anger.

"First, I will get my phone completely formatted then it shall be fine. Just like new. Then I will take care of my asshole cousins." He says to himself. He not for a second is thinking that he really must pay the ransom, or his phone will be destroyed. Not for a second, he is thinking that all the information on his phone will be made public. He is thinking that it is a virus and it can be fixed. He is already thinking of taking a half-day off and going to a phone repair shop to get this mess fixed. He stares at his phone once again hopelessly and sees the countdown is still on

11:10:43… 11:10:42… 11:10:41… and it continues.

While the person from Bangalore is desperate to get his phone fixed, the person from Delhi has boarded his train and is seated comfortably. It will take him forty minutes to reach his office. The train is lightly populated, there are only a few people standing. Some of them are sleeping but most of them are busy with smartphones.

He takes out his office laptop from the laptop bag and turns it on. He also takes out his headphones from the laptop bag and plugs into his ears and connects the other end to the phone. While the laptop is booting, he starts browsing through his WhatsApp messages. His phone is automatically connected to the free Wi-Fi network of the metro train.

After running through a few good morning messages in the family group, he turns his attention to his political party's cyber cell group named 'Cyber Soldier'. The first message in this group is a short video clip of about three minutes. The video clip shows a large screen with a projector inside a building that resembles a mosque. There are about a hundred chairs placed in front of this screen, it looks like a movie screening setup. There is a crowd of about a hundred to hundred and fifty men. All of them are wearing a skullcap and most of them are having a beard. They appear to be Muslim.

Few of them are standing, few of them are sitting on chairs.

On the screen, a cricket match between India and Pakistan is played. Pakistan is batting. The crowd is cheering on every run scored by the Pakistani team. At the end of the video when Pakistan team scores the final runs and wins the match, the crowd erupts in joy and celebration raising slogans

"Pakistan Zindabad..." "Zindabad... Zindabad... Pakistan Zindabad...".

Few men in the crowd are also flying Pakistan's flag. The incident in the video is claimed to happen in Mumbai.

"Bloody bastards!!!", he says cursing the Muslims after seeing the video.

Without a second thought, without checking any facts of the video, he forwards it to all other groups. Once the message is forwarded, there is no movement of his phone, he keeps moving his fingers on the touchscreen, but nothing happens. The phone is hung. But he is not at all surprised or panicked. His phone was behaving quite strangely from the past few days, after surviving a nasty fall from the office stairs. He keeps the phone inside his laptop bag, thinking that it will be back to normal after a few minutes.

Meanwhile, his laptop has started and is automatically connected to the metro train's free Wi-Fi. He logs on to his Facebook account, after wishing an office mate on his birthday, he quickly scrolls down and sees the same video which he forwarded in WhatsApp, shared by one of his friends. It's the same video but the only difference is, this time it claims that the incident took place in Hyderabad. To any reasonable person, the difference in a claim must have been enough to discredit the video. But the person from Delhi has given up reasoning when it comes to social media. He immediately shares the video on his Facebook page.

"Go to Pakistan, you blood-sucking parasites,", he comments on the video.

A few seconds after he has shared the video, the mouse pointer on the laptop screen suddenly flickers and stops moving. He keeps moving his fingers on the touchpad, but nothing happens. He presses ESC (escape) key multiple times but nothing happens. He shakes his head and reminds himself that it is an office laptop. He takes out his phone from the laptop bag to see if it has come back to normal functioning. He sees a message displayed on his phone

"YOU FORWARDED AN UNVERIFIED FALSE MESSAGE. YOU DIDN'T BOTHER TO CHECK IF MESSAGE WAS TRUE OR FALSE BECAUSE IT DOES NOT COST YOU ANYTHING. BUT TODAY YOU ARE GOING TO PAY"

But before he completes the reading, the message disappears, and another message starts scrolling

"YOUR PHONE WILL BE DESTROYED IN 12 HOURS ALL YOUR PRIVATE INFORMATION INCLUDING PICTURES, VIDEOS, EMAILS AND MESSAGES IN THIS PHONE WILL BE MADE PUBLIC"

The message stays on the phone screen for about twenty seconds and then another message starts scrolling

"IF YOU WANT TO STOP THIS PAY Rs.1,00,000 ACC NO 007511156375890 CRYPTO CODE: SSWIB0045617"

The message stays on the screen for a while, and the countdown continues

11:54:59… 11:54:58… 11:54:57… and it continues

Unlike the person in Bangalore, he is not panicked or shocked. He does not try to restart his phone. He is completely oblivious to the fact that he is in big trouble. He is thinking that it is a prank. He keeps the phone back in his laptop bag. He plans to use a spare phone kept in the office for a few days and will buy a new one over the weekend.

He now turns his attention to his office laptop which is still hung. He presses spacebar multiple times, Esc (escape) key multiple times, tries ALT+CTRL+DEL, tries ALT+F4 multiple times but nothing happens. He is about to give his laptop a hard restart by pressing the power button. He sees some movement of the mouse pointer. The screen flickers, the mouse pointer starts moving randomly in every direction. The screen flickering is very fast now. The mouse suddenly stops at the center of the screen. The screen flickering stops. For a few seconds, there is no movement. After a few seconds the mouse pointer starts growing, it covers half the screen in few seconds. It keeps growing and getting larger and covers the entire screen. The entire screen is covered by white. While all this was happening, the person from Delhi was just staring at the screen. Everything was happening so fast that he was not understanding anything. A message appears on the screen at once.

"YOU SHARED AN UNVERIFIED FALSE MESSAGE. YOU DIDN'T BOTHER TO CHECK IF MESSAGE WAS TRUE OR FALSE BECAUSE IT DOES NOT COST YOU ANYTHING. BUT TODAY YOU ARE GOING TO PAY"

The message stays on the screen for about ten seconds. He reads the complete message. He is calm and is smiling as he reads the message. The message disappears, and another message appears on his laptop screen.

"YOUR COMPUTER WILL BE DESTROYED IN 12 HOURS ALL YOUR PRIVATE INFORMATION INCLUDING PICTURES, VIDEOS, EMAILS AND MESSAGES IN THIS COMPUTER WILL BE MADE PUBLIC"

The message stays on the laptop screen for about twenty seconds and then another message starts scrolling

"IF YOU WANT TO STOP THIS PAY Rs.1,00,000 ACC NO 007511156375890 CRYPTO CODE: SSWIB0045617"

The message stays on the screen for a while, and the countdown continues

11:54:59… 11:54:58… 11:54:57… and it continues

Even after this message, he is not panicked. He has been pranked many times by his friends in many ways. He is habituated to pranks. He has been pranked by fake emails, gif files which will show that your inbox is getting copied to your boss's inbox or a picture of a lady in a swimsuit which will double itself whenever the close button is pressed. He is pretty sure this is one more prank. He simply presses the power button of his laptop located on the top right of the keyboard. He holds the power button for more than a minute so that the laptop completely shuts down. He turns on the laptop by pressing the same button, the laptop does not boot normally rather after some initial boot sequence, a blue screen appears and the same message scrolls again.

"YOU SHARED AN UNVERIFIED FALSE MESSAGE. YOU DIDN'T BOTHER TO CHECK IF MESSAGE WAS TRUE OR

FALSE BECAUSE IT DOES NOT COST YOU ANYTHING. BUT TODAY YOU ARE GOING TO PAY"

The message stays on the screen for about ten seconds. This time he is randomly pressing keys with both the hands. The message disappears, and another message appears on his laptop screen.

"YOUR COMPUTER WILL BE DESTROYED IN 12 HOURS ALL YOUR PRIVATE INFORMATION INCLUDING PICTURES, VIDEOS, EMAILS AND MESSAGES IN THIS COMPUTER WILL BE MADE PUBLIC"

The message stays on the laptop screen for about twenty seconds and then another message starts scrolling

"IF YOU WANT TO STOP THIS PAY Rs.1,00,000 ACC NO 007511156375890 CRYPTO CODE: SSWIB0045617"

The message stays on the screen for a while, and the countdown continues

11:54:59… 11:54:58… 11:54:57… and it continues

He frantically starts pressing random keys with both hands to stop the countdown. But the countdown continues. He is totally freaked out now, he starts sweating, his hands start shaking as if he is under a panic attack. Unable to do anything, he keeps staring at the screen helplessly.

He has realized that this is not a prank, it is something serious. He is thinking of consequences in the office. He swallows his saliva; his breathing has become very heavy. He is sweating on his forehead and back of his neck. He is feeling heaviness in his head and eyes. If he could have thought for one second and could have used his common sense instead of getting carried away in blind political affiliation before sharing the video, he could have saved himself from this humiliation.

He realizes now that his phone was also hung because he forwarded the same video, but he didn't understand as he was unable to read the complete message. He puts the screen of his laptop down, holding his phone in hand and clueless what to do next.

"I have confidential information on my office laptop about our clients, about their money, if that comes out, first I will be dead and then I will be fired." He says to himself

"I have to do something; I have to get my laptop fixed or I am dead", he says to himself and gasps for some air.

"And on my phone, I have messages of my girlfriend, my wife will kill me first and then divorce me later, the house I live in is on her name, after all, it was given by her dad. I am dead, I'm so dead right now." He says to himself, sweating profusely.

He tries to recall who had sent this message in the Cyber Soldier group; he doesn't remember. There are thousands of members in the Cyber Soldier group. He tries to recall who had shared this video on Facebook. He does not remember. In fact, until this moment he has never bothered to check who has forwarded this message or any message.

He doesn't know what to do. He is just sitting there wondering hopelessly. Thirty minutes have already passed, the train is nearing his station. He sees around him in the train most of the people using their smartphone trying to restart their phone looking worried and tensed. He thinks of asking if they are experiencing the same problem as he is experiencing with his phone and laptop, but everyone looks so shocked, angry and frustrated, he just keeps his mouth shut.

He quickly packs up all his belongings and hangs his laptop bag on his right shoulder while standing up from the seat. He starts slowly walking towards his right to take a sneak peek in all other passenger's smartphones. As he starts passing by each of the passengers who are either trying to restart their phones or staring their phones helplessly, he sees that everyone is seeing the same message of paying Rs.1,00,000 because they forwarded or shared an unverified false message and their phone will be destroyed in twelve hours. He also sees the same countdown on everyone's phone.

"I am not alone who is fucked up!!!" he says to himself in a sense of relief

"Many people are experiencing the same problem. That means many in my office must also be affected. I am not alone." He says to himself as the train approaches his station and he gets ready to get down without knowing what to do for his phone and office laptop.

Meanwhile, in Mumbai, the paid troll is ready to execute his next assignment. He is usually hired by political parties. His assignments are often to spread misinformation for the government or against the government. Unlike other social media trolls who just do it for pocket money and have no method in their trolling, being a professional social media troll, he has a well thought out trolling strategy.

He usually operates on Tuesdays and Thursdays. He has selected these days as Monday is a very busy day at work for everyone, Friday is the day when everyone is wrapping up and getting ready for the weekend and Wednesday is mid of the week hence people spend less time on social media. He has divided his day into three sections. 8 am to 11 am for twitter, where he is actively trolling using parody accounts. This is the time when people are commuting to the office and checking what is trending on twitter, and the troll gets maximum attention.

11 am to 12 noon, commenting on news articles and engaging in an argument in the comment section of news articles. This is the time when people have settled in office and browsing through google news, housewives have done with chores and are surfing the internet, college kids have a break, retired men are active on the internet and so on. 12.30 pm to 2.30 pm the office lunchtime when people are active on their Facebook and evening 5 pm to 9 pm back to tweeting again.

The modus operandi is simple. He receives a link to a google doc in his email by his employer. This google doc has about twenty to twenty-five messages articulating the same message but using different vocabulary and tone. The paid troll keeps using these messages with different parody account which he has already created. If one were to read these messages in the form of tweets, they appear to be tweeted by different people, but they are tweeted by one person, a paid social media troll. Later in the day, he uses a mixture of the same arguments and counterarguments on Facebook and news websites to engage other users in a dialogue.

But today he was about to meet the same destiny as the person in Bangalore and Delhi. As soon as he starts tweeting, he gets the same message he tweeted an unverified false message and he must pay Rs.1,00,000 else his phone or computer will be destroyed and all information in his phone will be made public.

Chapter 3

EMERGENCY MEETING

In the next two hours, this phenomenon spreads like wildfire. As an effect of this millions of social media users who were sharing or forwarding or tweeting unverified false information are on streets. There is chaos in every major city. Not only common man but Bollywood celebrities, cricketers, government officials, few ministers in power, few members of parliament, local leaders of all major political parties, famous writers, singers, so-called intellects, media personalities everyone is part of this chaos.

People are rushing in thousands to mobile repair shops or computer repair shops. Police stations are crowded for reporting complaints about demanding a ransom. In midst of all this chaos Home minister K R Dwarkanath also known as KRD has called an emergency meeting to review the situation.

He is a seasoned politician; he was a school principal before getting into politics. He is short about 5'4", bald-headed, green-eyed, he is wearing his frameless doubled lens glasses which he places on tip of his elongated straight nose while reading and near the eyes for seeing at distance, dressed in blue buttoned-up coat and white trousers.

He is sitting in a conference room which has a large c-shaped black office table and many chairs of white color. At the end of the room, in the center of the two edges of c shaped table is a projector and white screen. There are two LCD televisions on both the side walls. Home Minister K R Dwarkanath is seated in the middle. Towards his right Telecom minister Mr. Kulkarni, Facebook India head and his assistant, Twitter India head, and few other experts and advisors are seated.

Towards his left IT minister Mr. Hebbali, few other advisors and at the end National Cyber Defense Chief, retired air wing commander B. F. Magadi and his deputy Mr. Rajput are seated. Home Minister turns on the television on both the side walls with a press of a button on a remote. Every news channel is reporting live from each city, interviewing people.

"I just forwarded a heart touching story about Salman Khan and my phone got hung. It is a new phone which my husband had bought recently." The lady cries holding her phone standing in front of a mobile repair shop.

"I lost my job. I shared a Facebook post about our Prime Minister receiving UNESCO award using my office computer and it got infected" another man standing in front of the police station said.

"I will share whatever I want, it's my right, who the hell is this guy to hold me to ransom, I demand justice." another angry man screams standing in the crowd of thousands in front of a police station.

"These high-tech companies make billions of dollars, they are responsible for this, they should be made to pay." Says another senior gentleman.

"I have never seen anything like this, even after completely formatting the phone, it does not go away!!!" says a mobile repair technician.

"I had private pictures of me and my girlfriend, I already paid one lakh rupees. I will never, ever again forward any message!!!" said another youngster.

"What is the use of having such costly branded smartphone, I will start using a basic cell phone from today!!!" said another man

"What is our government doing?" asks another angry man.

And on and on, people continue to complain across different cities all over India.

Home minister KRD turns off the television with a press of a button on a remote. He is angry and frustrated. He removes his glasses and starts wiping them from a cloth, while he slowly keeps turning his chair towards his right, he fogs the glasses by breathing out on them and keeps wiping.

He gets up from his chair gently, turns his back towards everyone, while still wiping his glasses. There is absolute silence in the room.

 "What the hell is going on? Can anyone explain?" KRD asks in a very sharp voice. He pauses for a few moments expecting an answer while he wears his glasses back on. No one dares to answer, he looks around the room and continues.

 "We are a nation of 1.3 billion people, the largest democracy in the world. Even in the darkest hours of an emergency, we have defended freedom of speech and today millions of people across the country are held for ransom for expressing freely whatever they want to say," he says looking straight in the eyes of everyone in the room.

"What a shame!!! Can anyone explain what is happening… you Mr.IT minister or you Mr. Telecom minister or perhaps you guys pointing at Facebook India Head and Twitter India head?" He asks again.

Breaking the awkward silence and sensing KRD's frustration, Cybersecurity Chief B. F. Magadi speaks out

"We are under attack Sir!!!" he says in a firm voice just like expected from a retired air wing commander. B. F. Magadi is the no-nonsense straight forward guy. He became part of the cybersecurity team after he was forced to retire from the Indian Airforce due to an injury from the Kargil war. He was recently appointed as Cyber Defense Chief by the government. He is in his late forties; a thick handlebar mustache is a prominent feature of his face.

"We are under attack, Sir!!! A cyber-attack!!!" he repeats looking at home minister KRD

"What kind of cyber-attack? Didn't we had all the cyber defense in place, didn't we spend 400 crores of rupees in strengthening nations cyber security?" KRD asks

"Yes Sir, we did, and I assure you that nation's cyber defense is impenetrable but this is first and one of a kind of cyber-attack, where government or nation's defense forces are not attacked rather social media platforms used by every common man are attacked. Since these social media platforms are private tech firms, we are unaware of their security systems," B. F. Magadi replies.

"So, we spent crores on safeguarding nation's military secrets and left the common man on his own, vulnerable and insecure in these multibillion-dollar tech firms". KRD says sarcastically looking at Facebook India Head and Twitter India Head.

"What you have to say about all this Mr. Facebook?" asks KRD.

"Ahem…" Mr. Natarajan, Facebook India head clears his throat and swallows and leans forward to answer KRD. He resembles veteran cricketer Krishnamacharya Srikanth but without French beard. He is in his early fifties, having a jet-black head full of hair which is very unusual these days. He is wearing a sky-blue collarless half sleeve t-shirt with a Facebook logo on it. He has pressed his thick wide eyebrows into a frown.

"Sir… We are looking into the matter, all our security experts are working, here in India and back in the United States. We are on it." Mr. Natarajan replies

"It's a direct attack on our democracy. When people are held for ransom for expressing their views, it is the end of democracy, do you understand that Natarajan?" asks KRD.

"Yes Sir, I do, I am fully aware of the seriousness of the matter and I assure you that we are doing everything needed to resolve this issue," Mr. Natarajan replies.

"How is this even possible? you are the largest social media platform, you have billions of users across the world, you are like a parallel democracy, you have the power to topple governments, you can make a star out of a common man or break a star and make him a common man but yet you leave yourself open to such attacks. What the hell is your security about," KRD asks raising his voice in frustration.

"Sir… we take security very seriously and spend millions of dollars on it. In fact, security has been our largest expenditure in the past few years. But we cannot possibly predict and protect ourselves from every attack. We are working on it and it is just a matter of time. We will resolve this." Mr. Natarajan replies.

"It is only a matter of time, he says, a matter of time…" Home minister KRD smiles sarcastically looking at B. F. Magadi and pointing his hand at Mr. Natarajan.

"Everything is just a matter of time before we are late, and everything is lost… isn't it Natarajan." KRD pauses for a while and then continues to talk looking at Mr. Magadi.

"Anyway…, Magadi, what are we doing from our side to resolve this?" asks KRD

"We are working in collaboration with all these social media companies and till now here is what we can figure out," B. F. Magadi replies.

"Rajput… can you give more details on our findings," he says to his deputy S M Rajput.

Mr. Rajput came to National Cyber Defense a few years earlier. He had served in Mumbai, Delhi, and Bangalore's Cyber Crime Police Department prior to this. He is in his late thirties; He is about 5'6", athletic body, square face with short hair. His horseshoe mustache and a pale red colored birthmark which extends from his left eyebrow to the center of his cheek are prominent features of his face. He is wearing a plain blue shirt and Khaki pants.

"Sir… Yes…" He replies while connecting his laptop to the

projector screen and projects an animation showing the behavior of a ransomware attack.

"This is a ransomware attack, specifically targeting social media platforms. We still don't know the origin of the attack. As of now…" Before Mr. Rajput could complete, the IT minister seated beside KRD asks hesitantly.

"Ran… som… ware, what is that?"

"Sir, like criminals, hold people hostage and demand ransom to release them, this particular computer virus holds user's data as a hostage and demands to pay ransom to get the data back, hence the name ransomware. In this case, attackers are asking to pay Rs.1,00,000 within twelve hours of time else the data will be made public and the device either the effected cell phone or computer will be destroyed. Ransomware attacks are not new in the digital world, in past a Ransomware called 'WannaCry' had created similar chaos across the United States." Mr. Rajput pauses for a few moments looking around the room and continues

"But what makes this attack very dangerous is that it is specifically targeted on social media users. In past ransomware have exploited security loopholes in operating systems or have come in as an attachment in the email. But this time ransomware has disguised itself as a Facebook post or a WhatsApp forward or a tweet." He pauses for a few moments, looks around the room and continues.

"More specifically, the ransomware is targeting users who are either sharing or forwarding or tweeting false unverified information, fake news or hoaxes. As of now only users in India are affected."

"Any specific computer or cell phone brand which is targeted?" asks another advisor in the room.

"No Sir, no one is spared, costly and reputed brand to cheap duplicate phones, everyone is infected. Samsung, iPhone, Nokia, Oppo everyone. Desktop and laptops operating on Windows or iMac or any other operating system. Cell phone subscribed with Airtel or Jio or BSNL or any other network it does not matter," Mr. Rajput replies.

"Also, to be noted that right now only Facebook, Twitter, and WhatsApp are under attack. Other social media platforms like LinkedIn, Tinder, SnapChat, Instagram, TikTok, and few others are working fine," Mr. Rajput says.

"Do we know the origin of this thing?" asks KRD who is now seated on his chair

"No Sir…, as I was saying earlier that we don't know the origin of this ransomware and due to the privacy policies of these social media platforms we are unable to access all the needed information to track the origin." Mr. Rajput replies.

"A computer virus has held our freedom in hostage and you guys are concerned about your privacy policy. What the hell Natarajan," yells KRD in frustration.

"Sir, tracing any message back to its first occurrence, is impossible. Even if we were to discard our privacy policy and handover all the needed user information to the government, it will be of no use. It is impossible to trace the origin." Mr. Natarajan explains.

"So, what do you suggest then, surrender to this lame piece of shit, which has bought our country to a standstill," KRD asks.

"Mr. Magadi, did we get any information on the account number to which the ransom money needs to be transferred", asks Mr. Natarajan.

"What account number?" KRD asks

"Sir... this one..." Mr. Rajput points to the projector. On the projector, a part of ransomware's alert message is displayed in large and bold fonts

"PAY Rs.1,00,000 ACC NO 007511156375890 CRYPTO CODE: SSWIB0045617"

"Yes, this one, did we find anything about it?" asks Mr. Natarajan.

Before Mr. Rajput could answer, Mr. Magadi replies

"The account number belongs to World Crypto Bank. World's one and only Crypto Currency bank located in Tallinn, capital of Estonia, a small country in Europe."

"Cryp...to... Bank... what kind of bank is that," asks the IT Minister, hesitantly.

"Like we have banks for our daily usage of money in Indian currency, Crypto Bank allows its customers to hold their money in any legal Cryptocurrency. Customers can bring in money of any international currency and convert them into any cryptocurrency like Bitcoin," says Mr. Magadi.

"So that means all the money this ransomware is collecting is getting converted to cryptocurrency and moving outside the country," says KRD.

"Yes Sir..." Mr. Magadi replies.

"Icing on the cake, what more can go wrong, is there anything worse than this, I should know?" KRD asks.

"We don't know who the account holder is. Neither the bank will give us this information, nor we have any diplomatic arrangement with Estonia to force them to give us this information. Even if we navigate through international diplomacy, which by the way is very unlikely, it will be very late, and we may never know who the account belongs to." Mr. Magadi replies.

"Wonderful..." KRD says sarcastically and continues

"Our nation is hacked, millions of people are held hostage, open international money laundering is going on, we cannot trace the origin of the virus and we don't know anything apart from a puny account number. I have never felt so helpless..."

"I am sure Pakistan has its involvement in this!!!" says Telecom Minister.

Mr. Magadi smiles, while gently brushing his handlebar mustaches with his fingers and says

"Sir… it may be in your political advantage to blame Pakistan for everything. But the fact remains that this is a highly sophisticated attack. Pakistan is nowhere capable of carrying out such a sophisticated cyber-attack. They neither have resources nor guts to do so."

"Perhaps it may be China!!!" says another advisor in the room.

"China may be a suspect. In past Chinese hackers have targeted large corporations in the United States. They are very much capable. And if the ransomware destroys the phones and computers as it says, then China will be the main benefactor as there will be a sudden and very massive demand for mobile phones and computers which are mainly made in China. But given the international political environment and trade tension with the United States, China better not mess with us. But we can't be sure until we get some kind of lead." replies Mr. Rajput.

"Or it can be ISIS or Indian Mujahidin or the Anti National opposition party!!!" says Telecom Minister Mr. Kulkarni

"Stop it...Stop now... Kulkarni, this all sounds good only on your favorite news channel not here." warns KRD

"Sorry sir got carried away for a second," Mr. Kulkarni says apologetically.

"It can be anyone. We don't know anything right now." Mr. Magadi says. There is silence in the room for a while. Everyone is shocked, frustrated, angry and depressed. A sense of helplessness and anxiety is looming in the room.

"We must focus on a solution, not the problem." A calm resonating female voice breaks the silence. It is the Twitter India Head and only female in the room Miss. Annapurna. All this time she was just listening patiently as if she was allowing everyone to vent their frustration and anger. She has very strange calmness in her voice which is rather unusual for a stressful situation like this.

She comes from a print media background. She started as a journalist and went on to win Pulitzer award for her book "Unsung heroes of Indian Media", she later managed newsrooms of various reputed media houses in India and now working with Twitter. No doubt she has learned to manage stress. She is wearing a blue lady jacket with a white top inside.

Hair neatly made into a single pony that is reaching till the middle of her back. Large gold earrings are simple but elegant. She reminds of yesteryear actress Zeenat Aman.

"It doesn't matter who has done this, it may be China, or ISIS or our favorite Pakistan, we can figure it out later" she says, as everyone is listening attentively.

"The need of the hour is to stop this chaos from spreading further." She pauses for a few moments.

"We are wasting valuable time by discussing the origin of this ransomware. It is a computer virus. A computer virus and is no different from a biological virus. It shares the same traits; one spreads from person to person the other spreads from a computer to computer. So, the solution to this problem must be similar to what we could have done in case there was an H1N1 (Swine Flu) outbreak." She says in a very calm and composed manner. The pacing of her words is slow and clear. Her tone, as though she is explaining a very complex theory to a 5-year-old.

"Quarantine… prevent… and vaccinate…" KRD replies looking at Miss. Annapurna.

"Exactly!!!" She replies with some excitement.

"As the first step, we must stop this virus from spreading further." She says.

"Correct, you are absolutely correct. So, tell me now, how we should stop this virus from spreading?" asks KRD.

"From what we know till now only three platforms are infected, Twitter, Facebook, and WhatsApp. We also know that the ransomware is majorly affecting users who are sharing or forwarding unverified false messages or fake news. Also, not to forget the ransomware has given only twelve hours of time before it starts making the data public and destroying phones and computers. Out of these twelve hours, two hours thirty minutes have already gone. We are remaining with only nine hours thirty minutes. The ransomware has been active for 150 minutes and we are not able to understand anything about this ransomware. We don't know how it is detecting that messages are false or fake news. We don't know if it is exploiting a loophole in operating systems of these mobile phones and computers. We don't know if it's using bots to spread or is it using a single common security flaw in all our social media platforms. All we know is a Crypto bank account number… that's it." Miss. Annapurna says without losing her calm. After a moment of pause, she continues.

"At Twitter, we are working very hard to find out how to kill this ransomware and I am sure Facebook is also doing the same. But the fact is that we need more time. Until then the only way to stop this ransomware from spreading further is to immediately suspend services of Twitter, Facebook, and WhatsApp temporarily in India." she pauses for a moment. Everyone is listening to her very carefully.

"Our domestic rivalries, our business competition will always be there, we can settle that some other time. This is a very serious and big problem. If we do not resolve this, it is the end of social media platforms. This is it. This is it." She says.

"But…suspending the servi…" before Mr. Natarajan could complete his sentence, KRD intervenes

"Shh……" he says, pointing his finger towards Mr. Natarajan.

"You continue, please…" he says looking at Miss. Annapurna.

"We alone cannot handle this big problem. We must divide and conquer. My team and Mr. Natarajan's team together will tackle the technical aspect of this virus whereas Mr. Magadi's team can track down the responsible party for this chaos. We will collaborate and open doors to Mr.Magadi's team to hunt these culprits and Mr.Magadi's team will give access to their recently upgraded military supercomputer and ultra-high-speed servers so that we can analyze the data faster and nail down the solution quicker." She concludes.

There is silence in the room, everyone is looking at each other. Mr. Natarajan is annoyed. His disagreement with Miss. Annapurna's proposal is visible. While Mr. Magadi is also shaking his head in disagreement whereas Mr. Rajput seems to agree. IT minister and Telecom minster are still trying to understand the meaning of words Miss. Annapurna has spoken. Other advisors in the room are quiet, just staring at each other. The decision rests with KRD. KRD runs his eyes across the room.

"I agree with the young lady…" says KRD

"Sir but allowing private firms to access our servers will compromise the nation's security," says Mr. Magadi with frustration.

"Sir… we cannot allow the government to access the user's personal information, it will be a breach of our privacy policy." Says Mr. Natarajan.

"Magadi… Natarajan… didn't you hear what she said? Magadi, this is a national emergency, millions of people are held hostage. If we cannot bail out our people from this crisis to hell with protecting military secrets. Natarajan, as she said, this is doomsday for social media, what good will be your privacy policy if your platform sieges to exist. It's in everyone's best interest right now that we work together." He pauses for a moment and continues

"Magadi… you nail the bastards behind this. Natarajan and Miss. Annapurna, you guys get to your work and keep updating me every hour. Come what may, at the end of twelve hours I want everything back to normal." KRD pauses for a while.

"Hebbali… Issue immediate orders to suspend services of Facebook, Twitter, and WhatsApp until further notice." KRD says to IT minister Mr. Hebbali.

"Yes… Sir" he replies. KRD presses a button on the intercom phone located in front of him.

"Murthy… I will talk to the press in fifteen minutes, inform everyone."

"Yes… Sir… all are waiting for the past two hours." Mr. Murthy replies.

Home Minister K R Dwarkanath disconnects the call, stands up from his chair and says

"Gentlemen and the lady, I generally end meetings with a thank you or best of luck. But today, neither I will thank you nor wish you the luck. I know very well that luck will not save us today and I will thank you only if we succeed and if we fail, then this will be the darkest day our nation has ever witnessed. It is 11 am, we have nine more hours to go before it is the end of freedom of speech and democracy. Let's get to work now."

KRD concludes the meeting and leaves the room. IT minister and Telecom Minister exit the room along with other advisors. Mr. Magadi, Rajput, Natarajan, and Miss. Annapurna discuss among themselves regarding further actions.

Chapter 4

FORENSIC CYBER PSYCHOLOGIST

Mr. Magadi and Mr. Rajput are seated in their car and heading back to their National Cyber Defense headquarters.

"Rajput… how are we going to do this? Mr. Magadi asks, while gently brushing his handlebar mustaches with his fingers.

"Infront of KRD we committed to trace the culprits in less than nine hours, even if we get access to all data from Facebook and Twitter, you and I both know it's impossible to trace the origin…" Mr. Magadi says.

"I know that Sir… but I also know someone who can really help us in this crisis…" answers Mr. Rajput

"Who… I don't know anyone in our department who can do this… who is it?" asks Mr. Magadi

"Professor Fabulous!!!" he replies

"Who…" Mr. Magadi asks once again.

"Professor Fabulous…Sir…, he is an expert in Forensic Cyber Psychology and Professor of Industrial-Organization Psychology at Bangalore University. While I was working in the Police department on Cyber Crimes, he had helped us to resolve many cases, I am sure, his expertise and experience in this field will be really useful" he replies.

The moment Mr. Rajput said Professor and Psychology together Mr. Magadi imagined of a wearied, socially awkward, unfriendly, idiotic intellectual academic who will have nothing but unrealistic solutions which suit only to the ideal scenario. That's how Mr. Magadi perceived any academic or intellectual.

"Fabulous… what a strange and unusual name. I have never heard of him," Mr. Magadi says with a lot of skepticism.

"Sir… he was here yesterday for a conference… and probably still in town…" Mr. Rajput says while unlocking his iPad which he is holding in his hand. He quickly opens the YouTube app and goes to his favorite list and plays a video and says.

"Sir… watch this…" he gives his iPad to Mr. Magadi. A YouTube video titled "India Conclave 2019: Professor Fabulous" starts playing. In the video, there is a typical conference setup. There is a neatly arranged stage. A large digital projection that keeps displaying India Conclave 2019 animation. There is a clear acrylic podium on the left of the stage with India Conclave 2019 poster on it.

The host of the conference, a prominent news anchor is standing at the podium.

"Welcome back all… can everyone quickly settle down; we have a very interesting man with a very interesting topic coming up next" he says looking at the audience. After a few moments of indistinct chatter and few murmurs, the room goes silent, it gets darker, and the light is focused on the podium.

"Welcome to the last session of today's conference and as every year we save the best for the last." The host says looking at the audience and the TV camera placed right in front of him.

"Generally, I start by saying the cliché line 'The man needs no introduction' and go on to give a long-detailed introduction of the speaker…" he says, smiling at the camera. The audience also giggles.

"Our next speaker specifically asked me, not to give a long introduction about him. But as per formality, I will start by saying 'the man needs no introduction'" the audience bursts into laughter and Mr. Magadi also smiles.

"He is the one and only Forensic Cyber Psychologist of India. He has helped to resolve many cybercrimes not only in India but across the world. He has published numerous papers, articles, and studies related to human online behavior. His recently published book 'The Veil of Social Media' is a worldwide sensation. Please welcome with a round of applause Professor Fabulous!!!" There is applause by the audience as the host gets down from the stage. The animation on the screen stops and on top of the screen it reads "India Conclave 2019" in the middle it reads "Fake News and Social Media" and in the next line it reads "By Professor Fabulous".

 A man enters the room from the right side of the stage, with slow but very firm steps holding a small remote in his hand. He is dressed in a denim blue jean, a white shirt which is very neatly tucked in and a blue double-breasted blazer. A brown leather belt and dark brown leather shoes which look brand new. He is lean and about six feet tall. He appears very strong and rugged. He has an oblong face with a short but dense beard, thick mustache. His beard covers half of his face. The beard is a mix of grey and black. Similarly, his thick mustache is a mix of black and grey. He has a Lenin nose, which is broad, much like an inverted triangle with flared nostrils and a sharp tip at the end. He has deep black eyes that feature an extra layer of skin that droops over the crease, causing the eyelid to appear smaller. Wide eyebrows. Big forehead, curly black and grey head full of short dense hair. He gets wrinkles around his eyes when he smiles. Professor Fabulous, like his name, is just fabulous. His personality is gripping.

"Thank you everyone…" he says standing at the center of the stage.

"I am Professor Fabulous, Forensic Cyber Psychologist. I usually start my talks by explaining the meaning of Forensic Cyber psychology and what is that I do. As the field is new and not everyone is familiar with it." He pauses for a few moments looking at the audience.

"But since it is the last session, and you have been a great audience all day long, I will start with a small demonstration to show how fake news spreads across social media…" he says. Mr. Magadi is watching and listening to the video very attentively.

"For this demonstration, I will use WhatsApp as an example. I will display four messages one by one and ask each one of you if you will forward the message. You can raise your hands if you will forward the message." He says looking at the audience.

"ok… is that clear…" he asks walking towards the podium. The audience nods in agreement.

"Ok… then, here is the first message…" he says by clicking the button on the remote. On the screen, the message is displayed. It is a picture of Indian business tycoon Late Dhirubhai Ambani. Below the picture, the message reads

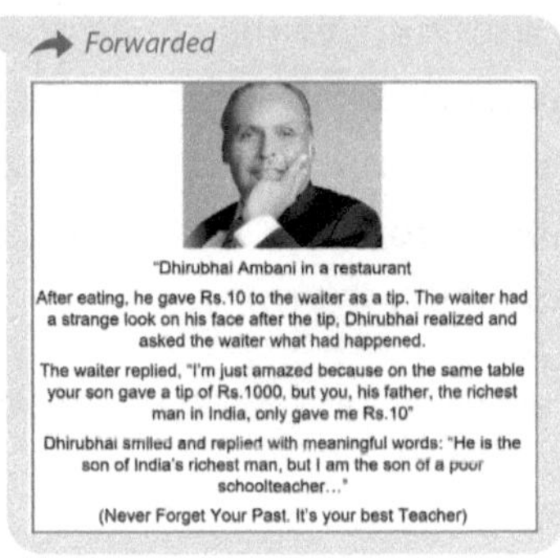

"Ok… how many of you will forward this message to various WhatsApp groups…" Professor Fabulous asks the audience.

"Show of hands please…" he says.

About sixty to seventy percent in the audience lift their hands agreeing that they will forward the message. After a few moments, Professor Fabulous continues

"Ok… here is the next one…" he says. The next message is displayed on the screen. It is a black and white old picture of Mahatma Gandhi dancing with a white foreign lady.

"Let's see… how many of you would like to forward this message…" asks Professor Fabulous looking at the audience. About forty to fifty percent of the audience lift their hands in agreement of forwarding the message.

"That's good… That's good…" he says nodding at the audience.

"Here is the next one…" he says, and the next message is displayed on the screen. It is a picture of an old one rupee note issued in 1917. The picture claims that in 1917 one rupee was equal to $13 USD and in 2014 $1 USD is equal to Rs.63.

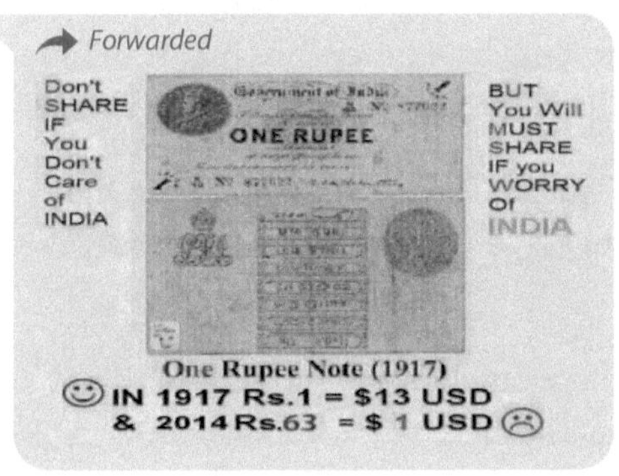

Before Professor Fabulous could ask, he sees that almost everyone in the room has lifted their hands in agreement that they will forward this message. One gentleman sitting in the left corner has raised both his hands.

"That's wonderful… you are such a great audience." Professor Fabulous says.

"Here is the last message, it's a video clip. Watch and raise your hands if you will forward the message," he says.

On the screen, a short video clip of about thirty-two seconds plays. On top of the video, the caption reads

"Eve teasers taught a lesson,"

 It's a video clip shot by a cell phone. In the video, a woman dressed in jogging attire is chasing a man. Another woman who is not seen in the video but is only heard in the background is capturing the video. The man dressed in a short T-shirt and jeans is running away from a woman. The man is trying to cover his face by bike helmet. After chasing the man for a few seconds, the woman catches up with the man. She starts abusing him and asks him to kneel. The man keeps apologizing. Once the man kneels, the woman kicks him on the face while abusing him. Few bystanders are just watching. After two or three kicks the man gets up and runs away and the video stops.

"So… that was the last message. How many will forward this video message? Show of hands please…" says Professor Fabulous.

Almost all the women in the room raise their hands. Few men also raise their hands.

"Thank you… thank you all for being such a wonderful audience" Professor Fabulous says as he walks to the center of the stage, the screen behind him shows all the four messages.

"You all chose to either forward or not to forward these messages. I want to ask all of you, why?" he pauses for a moment.

"Why did you choose to forward or not forward these messages… anyone? anyone???" he asks.

A man raises his hand to answer the question.

"No need to raise hands or stand up, you can answer from your seats," Professor Fabulous says.

"I chose to forward the story of Dhirubhai Ambani because I liked the moral of the story," says the man.

"I chose to forward the last video message so that thousands of girls who face eve-teasing in India will get encouraged and stand up against this evil." says another lady.

"I chose to forward the second message because M.K Gandhi is the reason why we are like this today; we could have been better off without him," says another man.

"I chose not to forward any of these messages because I have already seen and forwarded these messages once." another man says.

"I chose to forward the 3rd message, to spread awareness about how corrupt and incompetent people in power have looted our country," says another man

"I chose to forward 3rd message because I am Indian," says another man.

"I chose not to forward any of these messages because they are all boring," says another man.

"Ok… Ok… thank you… thank you…" Professor fabulous stops the audience from responding further.

"This is how precisely fake news and misinformation spreads like wildfire. It is not the bots or paid trolls or creators of fake news. It is us, who chose to forward, share or tweet the messages, stories, pictures, videos which appeal to our emotion, which validate our beliefs, which matches our bias or opinions. Confirmation bias, it is called…" he says and pauses for a few seconds.

"We don't care about facts, we don't care about the credibility of the sources, we don't reason, we don't question, we just spread the word." Professor fabulous says looking straight into the eyes of the audience.

"Here in India, we love to share everything, from our food to clothes, to houses, to beds, to cigarettes, to teas, to drinks. Sharing is caring, this is in our DNA, we are obsessed with sharing." He pauses for few seconds as audience giggles

"You will share if you care. That's what we inherently believe. But we have to start caring before sharing else sooner or later we will all become a victim of fake news." he pauses and continues again.

"We should start caring about the authenticity of the messages about their truthfulness before we share them. Had we cared; we could have not chosen to forward any messages I showed you. The first message about Late Dhirubhai Ambani is false, which is a copy of a similar fake story that originated in the United States about Bill Gates. Since then its making rounds on social media about different personalities. The second picture I showed is not of Mahatma Gandhi, but of an actor who is playing the role of Mahatma Gandhi. Likewise, the remaining two messages are also false. But these messages appealed to our emotions. Had we kept emotions away and reasoned, questioned these messages then we could have not acted as we did." He pauses.

"In a true sense this issue is not new, fake news existed in the past and it will continue to exist until human civilization exists. What is new about this… is the way people have reacted to these and the way technology has enabled fake news and hate speech to spread like wildfire. Today we live in a world where people believe in whatever they want to believe and use the flimsiest piece of evidence to justify that belief, even when there is plenty of verified evidence to disprove it. It has become almost impossible today to separate fact from fiction," He pauses for few seconds and continues.

"This all started with a potent mixture of three most incredible and most important inventions of the 21st century. The Internet, Smart Phone and Social Media. These are the new food, clothe and shelter of today's life. Knowingly or unknowingly we have made our systems, our digital infrastructure and our lives so much dependent on these three items, that living without them is impossible and impractical. I will take you a few decades back when the internet was not invented. The conspiracy theories, hoaxes, rumors existed even then. If you remember the famous hoax or scam in India was spread by postcards. People received a postcard from an anonymous sender. The postcard read that you are cursed by some deity, you must send similar postcards to a hundred other people to rescue yourself from the curse. If you ignore this, bad luck will strike and something bad is going to happen to you or your loved ones. Innocent honest God-fearing people wrote hundreds of such postcards believing what they have read and thus the chain continued." He pauses for a few seconds and continues.

"Before the internet such hoaxes, conspiracy theories were very limited. There was no practical and efficient way of spreading these kinds of falsehood. It remained within the region or community. Occasionally a conspiracy theorist is to publish a book or small pamphlet that had limited reach and life. These falsehoods never reached regular households. They never were backed by mainstream media. Either the print media or television media." Professor fabulous is moving around the stage as he is speaking. The audience is listening to him very attentively.

"After the invention of the internet, conspiracy theorists, hoax creators, scammers and other voices which could not make it to mainstream media found one large and open platform to put their point across. Most of them just wanted to earn some money, get some popularity and attention of the world and few genuinely believed in what they are publishing is the truth. Anyone, without any credentials, without any proof, without citing any sources could go and publish anything. Even then the reach and life of these hoaxes were very limited since the internet should be accessed through computers and only people having access to and knowledge of computers will indulge with the internet. Even for people who are computer literate, unless they were interested in these conspiracy theories and looked for these on the internet, they would never know about its existence. Neither there was an efficient and easy way to spread the word to other internet users. In the Indian context, the percentage number of entire populations having access to computers and the internet could be in single-digit or even less than that in the late nineties and early two thousand. This restricted and limited the spreading of hoax or fake news unless they were endorsed by mainstream media either print or television." He pauses for a few seconds and continues.

"With the invention of the smartphone, the internet reached every household and every common man's world. I am using specifically the word "smartphone" not "cell phone" or "mobile phone" on purpose. Even though the cell phone was invented much earlier than a smartphone and was getting used heavily for communication, it was not until it was re-invented as the smartphone it rose to prominence. The smartphone became the next big thing and had reached almost every household. Having simple and easy internet access it opened flood gates for many hoax creators, fake news media outlets and many others who wanted to reach every household. Even after this the reach and life of a hoax were restricted. Smartphones gave easy and convenient access to the internet but still no efficient way to share or spread the hoax. Both cell phones and smartphones had messaging services, through which text and picture messages can be circulated but the reach was limited. Few political parties in India had already realized the potential of this and already started using SMS (Short messaging services) for communication or miscommunication or spreading rumors. But the reach was still limited." He pauses for a moment and continues.

"Now came The Social Media. The invention of social media changed the very notion of truth on this planet. The shortcoming of smartphones and the internet of not being able to spread the information to every household was addressed by social media. The power of social media was that it connected everyone. No matter where you came from, no matter what you believed in or not believed in, everyone willingly or unwillingly became part of Social Media. Social Media also addressed one very important factor, I am not sure if it was by design or it was by mistake, but it allowed all kinds of unvetted information to reach its users. Doesn't matter if the user wants it or not… it's on your social media page. With just one click of a button and within a few seconds the information reaches millions of users. You can love it or hate it, but you cannot ignore it. This was the last pillar on which entire fake news, hoax creators, conspiracy theorists built their empires. "A Smartphone", the device which everyone carries, "The Internet", the medium on which all the digital information can be transmitted and more importantly its affordable and "The Social Media", the open platform on which anybody can share, spread any information. The device, the medium and the platform made this a complete package that can be used by anyone to turn the world upside down." Professor Fabulous says in the video.

This is the first time Mr. Magadi has heard Professor Fabulous. He is listening and watching the video very attentively. An annoying ad disrupts his involvement. He hands over the iPad back to Mr. Rajput

"He is good… isn't it Sir?" Mr. Rajput asks.

"Hm…Rajput… to be honest I do not have any respect for academics and intellectuals who live in comfort and keep proposing unrealistic solutions for everything." Mr. Magadi replies and pauses for a second and looks Mr. Rajput directly into his eyes and says.

"But… I trust you and your judgement… Do you trust him…"

Mr. Rajput doesn't answer immediately but after a few seconds he says

"I trust his work… I have worked with him before… He is the best person at the moment for this situation…"

"I sense some skepticism in your voice… but I will trust you and believe that you understand the seriousness and depth of this crisis more than me…" Mr.Magadi says and pauses for a few seconds looking outside through the window brushing his mustaches with the back of his fingers. The car stops in front of their headquarters.

"Get him… Professor whatever… Get in touch with him…" Mr. Magadi says and gets down from the car.

"Yes… Sir… I will get in touch with him as soon as possible." Mr. Rajput says and starts looking for Professor Fabulous phone number on his phone.

Chapter 5

THE FIRST LEAD

Professor Fabulous is slowly getting out of his deep sleep, he is not completely awake neither completely asleep, a state of morning fuzziness. The tableside phone in his hotel room has been ringing continuously for the last forty minutes, but it hasn't bothered him. After the conference yesterday, at the dinner table, he had met a lot of new people and engaged in interesting discussions. He was so engrossed in discussions that he didn't realize that he already had multiple cocktails. He kept eating something or the other until the restaurant closed. And finally, he had one large whiskey, that one final drink after heavy eating sphere had made him very dizzy, he vaguely remembers coming in the room and going to sleep immediately.

The tableside phone keeps ringing, as he is slowly waking up from his sleep. The phone ring sounds like it was ringing somewhere far away. He rolls up his eyes lazily. The phone ring gets louder and clearer as Professor sheds his sleep from his brain. He sits up in his bed, still feeling very lame and lethargic from last night's heavy dinner, still lazy to pick the phone.

Finally, after getting annoyed by continuous phone rings, he extends his right arm towards the phone, but he can't reach it. He is too lazy to get up, but the phone ring is annoying him, he moves towards the right by shifting his entire body and stretches his arm again. He is about to pick up the phone, but the phone ring stops at once. He looks at the phone strangely as if it was ringing to only wake him up. He is still seated in his bed just staring at the wall. There is the knock on the door.

"rat-a-tat-tat…. rat-a-tat-tat…" it sounds like machine gunfire. Professor Fabulous is still very lazy to get up and answer the door. He keeps sitting on his bed without responding to the door knock.

"rat-a-tat-tat… rat-a-tat-tat…" the door knocks again but louder this time.

Scratching his beard with his fingers Professor shouts

"Who is it?" There is no immediate answer but after a few seconds a female voice replies

"Professor Fabulous there is an emergency phone call for you, it is from your office. Please pick up the table side phone."

"What… Hotel is on emergency…" says the professor not understanding the complete message.

"Emergency phone call for you. Please pick up the phone," the female voice says this time louder.

"Ok…ok…I got it" says the professor.

"Emergency… what emergency" he says, as he starts getting up from the bed. He pushes the blanket and the comforter away and sits up at the side of the bed with his feet on the floor. He has not even removed the sock from yesterday's conference. He looks at the digital clock placed beside the table phone. The time is 10.20 am. His mobile phone is beside the table phone which he had kept in silent mode. He gets up from the bed and picks up his mobile phone.

He sees 112 missed calls from known numbers, 76 missed calls from new numbers, multiple text messages. He doesn't know what has happened.

"What is going on, is there a terrorist attack or earthquake or something!!!" he says to himself while browsing through the missed call list.

"bring… bring… bring… bring" the table side phone rings again.

"bring… bring…bring…" He lifts the phone and before he could say hello, a panicky voice says

"Sir… Hombal here…" Hombal works for Professor Fabulous as a research assistant in university.

"Sir… where are you… I have been trying your number since last forty minutes," he says.

"I just overslept… why… what is wrong…" says Professor hesitantly.

"Don't you know what has happened?" he asks.

"No… what has happened… I don't know. I just woke up," replies Professor.

"My God!!! turn on the TV and see for yourself" before the professor could say anything Hombal disconnects the call.

"Hello... Hello... Hombal... hello... what the hell" professor keeps the phone down and looks towards the flat screen LCD TV located in front of his bed. He quickly grabs the remote from the dressing table located below the TV and turns on the TV.

"India under-attack, this is the worst cyber-attack the world has witnessed. This is the 9/11 of the cyber world" the reporter on the TV screams. Professor changes to a few other news channels and tries to understand what has happened, but all he can hear is screaming and shouting reporters without giving accurate information. He mutes the TV and throws the tv remote on the bed and starts browsing on his phone. He opens the YouTube app and quickly goes to the notifications, as expected his favorite freelance journalist has uploaded a quick four-minute video explaining the whole issue without any screaming, without any overloaded animations. After watching the video, he realizes that Facebook, Twitter, and WhatsApp are down. As he tries to find out more by searching on google, reading through a few articles, he gets a call from Mr. Rajput.

Professor Fabulous is hesitant to lift Mr. Rajput's call. His association with Mr. Rajput had ended on a very bitter note and since then both had not spoken. Mr. Rajput had first met Professor Fabulous about fifteen years ago when he was training under Alok Kumar, then Deputy Commissioner of Police, Bangalore. Since then they had shared a very good respectful relationship. No matter where Mr. Rajput was posted during his career in the Police department, he always teamed up with Professor Fabulous to resolve many cyber crimes and rackets. Until four years ago due to Professor's overconfident and arrogant behavior which caused a lot of personal and professional harm to Mr. Rajput, their association had ended.

Professor Fabulous lifts the call after a few rings

"Rajput..." he says instead of hello.

"Where are you Professor, I have been trying your number since morning..." Mr. Rajput yells instead of greeting him and asking about his whereabouts and his health and family. And likewise, neither Professor Fabulous enquires about his health and family or his new job in National Cyber Defense and comes directly to the point and says.

"I came to know just now about the attack. Are you in your office?"

"Yes..." he replies

"Do you have any leads?" he asks

"No...nothing really, apart from the account number," Mr. Rajput replies

"Ok... I want you to go to Central Jail... right now..." he says.

"Central Jail!!!" Mr. Rajput replies

"Yes...Central Jail. Right now. Get permission from the Jail Warden to meet prisoner Manish Patel. Tell the Jail Warden specifically that Professor Fabulous wants to see Manish Patel and its matter of urgency" Professor Fabulous says.

"Who Manish Patel?" asks Mr. Rajput

"I will meet you in thirty minutes outside Central Jail, I will explain to you everything." Professor Fabulous pauses for a while and continues

"Rajput… This is not the first time… This has happened once before." He says.

"What!!!... when!!!… who!!!…"? asks Mr. Rajput with shock.

"Listen to me, we don't have time. Go to Central Jail and get permission to see Manish Patel and be ready by the time I arrive in thirty minutes," he says again.

"Ok… Ok… Manish Patel, Central Jail. I will start right now. See you in thirty minutes,"

"Good…" He replies

Professor Fabulous disconnects the call. He heads to the shower. 30 minutes later Mr. Rajput is waiting for Professor Fabulous in front of the Central Jail. An uber cab arrives, Professor Fabulous gets down from the cab and hurries towards Mr. Rajput. He is dressed in ash-colored, no collar shirt with long sleeves and no cuffs. A royal blue sleeveless jacket with its top 3 buttons open. A classic sky-blue denim jean which is reaching only till his ankles so that white socks can be seen. Dotted black round toe shoes, which is unusual as he always prefers to wear square toe shoes.

"Hello Rajput, come let's go…" he says, without stopping. They both head inside the jail, Mr. Rajput hands over the paperwork at the entrance.

Professor Fabulous is not new either to Manish Patel or to Jail Warden. Since Manish is serving his time for a Cyber Crime and Professor Fabulous being a Forensic Cyber Psychologist, he is studying Manish's case and is having interviews with him. As Mr. Rajput and Professor Fabulous walk inside the Jail, they are escorted to a small room where Professor Fabulous conducts his interviews. The room has nothing but a table and two chairs. Professor Fabulous is sitting on one chair doing something on the phone, while Mr. Rajput is standing holding a bunch of papers and his iPad. The other chair is vacant. Mr. Rajput is now getting impatient as there are thousands of questions in his mind. Professor Fabulous still doing something on his phone and without lifting his head says.

"Rajput… as usual, you must have many questions…"

"Yes Professor…" Mr. Rajput replies immediately and in very next second in one breath he says

"Do you mind… telling me what is happening and who is this Manish Patel, how is he related to this all… When this has happened before or will I be the blind mouse… until the very end when the mystery unfolds."

Having worked with Professor Fabulous in the past, Rajput is very aware of his working style. Professor Fabulous has two versions of himself, the first one is a Forensic Cyber Psychologist who never gives out any information until it is exclusively asked for and talks to the point. If you don't ask anything, he will not tell anything and at the end mystery unfolds, and you connect the dots by yourself. The second one is the Professor version who treats you like a student and gives a detailed explanation until you understand. Rajput had come to believe that even though Professor Fabulous does not admit it, he enjoys being a Professor rather than being a Forensic Cyber Psychologist. Even though he consciously tries to minimize the Professor version and tries to stick to the Forensic Cyber Psychologist version, sub-consciously the Professor version could have taken over him.

"Slow down... Slow Down... one by one..." says Professor Fabulous.

"Ok... First thing first... who is Manish Patel," asks Mr. Rajput

Professor Fabulous now gets up from his chair and leaves the phone on the table and says

"Manish Patel is our first key in this matter and will possibly lead us to the source of this attack. There is no point in trying to find a technical solution for this, whoever has done this, is too smart and has thought out any which way this can be stopped and has worked around it. The tech firms with all their engineering force will not be able to stop this. The only way to stop this will be to find the person or persons behind the attack."

"What does Manish Patel know?" asks Mr. Rajput

"Manish Patel has experienced this attack before. He was just like the pilot version of the project, which is used for testing before launching the main product" says Professor Fabulous.

"Ok... I am totally confused..." says Mr. Rajput

The Professor version of Professor Fabulous now kicks in and starts giving a detailed explanation

"Ok... Let's start from the beginning..." says Professor Fabulous

"Manish Patel as a kid dreamt of one and only one thing. Going to America and earning a lot of dollars. He was influenced by his relatives especially his uncle who was already a well-known motelier in the United States. After getting an Engineering degree in computer science, he did his MBA just for the sake of a master's degree to get a VISA for USA. But he knew very well that only education will never get him to the United States. He needed contacts. Apart from his uncle who he had visited twice in the United States, he had made friends with few investment bankers in the United States and had established a good rapport with them during his tourist visits. All this had helped in landing a job in the United States soon after his completion of an MBA. He got his H1B visa for three years and landed in the United States in 2014." Professor Fabulous stops for a while and looks at Mr. Rajput who is listening very carefully and then continues.

"Three years had passed. Manish was living life to the fullest. Nice job, good salary, nice car, beautiful and sexy Apexa Patel whom he was all set to marry in the next few months. Apexa was a US citizen, one of the reasons why Manish was marrying her so that he can get the green card and eventually US citizenship. Life was good and going as Manish had planned. But in November 2016 defying all odds, Donald Trump had won United States elections. Since then not only for illegal immigration, not only refuges but entire immigration process including legal immigration came under fire." Professor Fabulous pauses for a moment.

"And… Let me guess, Manish was denied VISA extension and had to return to India…" said Mr. Rajput.

"Good job Sherlock Holmes" replies Professor. He often referred Mr. Rajput as Sherlock Holmes or James Bond or Pink Panther to make fun of him to which Mr. Rajput never took any offense. He now is doing it intentionally to keep the mood light in the tense situation so that the stress of their bitter past does not intervene in their judgement. Mr. Rajput does not react, in the past, he could have giggled, but today he has a stone face expression to everything.

"If it was only denial or rejection, it was just a matter of time, Manish could have made it back to the United States after a few months with a new job offer. But it was not the case. United States Citizenship and Immigration Services (USCIS) had found out that he obtained his VISA through fraudulent means back in 2014. His job offer was through a bogus company which his investment banker friends had created. Manish had paid $10,000 for them to do this. As a result of this USCIS charged Manish with fraud, blacklisted him from re-entering the United States and deported him back to India." Professor Fabulous pauses.

"Sherlock Holmes… what happens next?" He says looking at Mr. Rajput to see if he loosens a bit… but there is no reaction from him.

"Obviously the marriage could have been called off… he must have been shamed by his relatives, his uncle who he had admired must have started hating him, his parents must have been ashamed of him …. on and on, but how is this all related to today's incident," Mr. Rajput asks

"Manish's American dream was shattered. Instead of seeking a new job, new life and new wife in India, which he could have done, he grew very bitter and decided that he will use all his skills, smartness and intelligence to take revenge on the United States. That's where he entered into Cyberspace." Professor paused for a while and continued.

"From his experience of living in the United States, he had arrived at few conclusions about Americans and the American lifestyle. He had concluded that in general Americans are very honest, law fearing and law-abiding citizens, but they are not smart people. Honest but not smart. It was easy to fool them or scam them. They valued truth, honesty and being kind but they didn't practice caution while doing so. Kind but not cautious. And finally, even though Americans claimed to have the highest privacy, most of the information related to them is available for free in the public domain either through social media or through some other means." before Professor Fabulous could say any further, a constable escorts Manish Patel into the room.

"Professorrrrrr…. Saab…" Manish says looking at Professor Fabulous.

"Hello, Manish… How are you" replies Professor Fabulous

"Right now, I am very uncomfortable in these handcuffs…" Manish says by placing his hands in front of his face and turning towards constable to open them. Constable looks at Professor Fabulous and Mr. Rajput seeking approval to open his handcuffs. Mr. Rajput signals the constable by nodding his head.

Chapter 6

THE SCAMMER

Manish Patel is a sweet, cute looking young man, with a very rude, over-confident attitude. He is about 5 feet 10 inches, a little overweight with a noticeable paunch. Fair complexion, clean shaved, neatly done head full of hair, parting from the left. Thick eyebrows are seen even after large glasses cover half of his face. A square nose is pressed by the weight of heavy glasses. Unlike other inmates, he is not dressed in jail attire. He is dressed in a nice yellow t-shirt and blue denim jeans along with a nice pair of canvas shoes. By far his appearance is very neat and clean given that fact he is in jail. Mr. Rajput is quite shocked to see an inmate serving jail time for a crime and having access to all normal life utilities.

"He must have bribed the Jail Warden," Mr. Rajput thinks standing quietly.

But Manish Patel didn't bribe Jail Warden, he made a deal with Professor Fabulous. For agreeing to co-operate with Professor Fabulous for his interviews he had demanded the VIP cell, which is usually for Politician's or any other political prisoners. This cell has a private bathroom, comfortable bedding, access to newspaper, permission to wear their clothes, weekly one phone call along with many other things.

"Professor Saab… I thought you are not going to visit for another month" says Manish taking few steps towards the vacant chair looking at Mr. Rajput

"Ya… that's correct, but something has come up urgently…" replies Professor Fabulous

"By the way… meet S M Rajput, he is from National Cyber Defense…" says Professor Fabulous pointing at Mr. Rajput

"Hello…" says Mr. Rajput and moves forward to shake his hand. Manish takes few steps forward towards Mr. Rajput as if he is going to shake his hand, but instead he snaps him and moves towards the vacant chair and says sarcastically

"National Cyber Defense wants to talk to a scammer…"

Professor Fabulous looks at Mr. Rajput and signals him not to react by winking his eye.

"Manish… There was a cyber-attack on social media platforms this morning. Facebook, Twitter, and WhatsApp are down. Almost everyone using these apps are infected. Take a look at this…" Professor Fabulous says in a serious tone and grabs the iPad from Mr. Rajput. He opens the YouTube app and quickly goes to the same four minutes video from his favorite freelance journalist explaining the whole issue without any screaming, without any overloaded animations. He places the iPad on the table, takes his phone which he left on the table while talking to Mr. Rajput. Meanwhile, Manish has already pulled the chair and seated placing his hands on the table. Manish picks up the iPad in his hands and starts watching the video with complete attention without blinking his eyes. As the video progresses his complete demeanor and body language changes from over-confident to dull and depressing. His shoulders have gone low, he is breathing slowly, eyes have gone red. After he is done watching the video, he places the iPad on the table. Professor Fabulous who now is standing behind him places his hand on his shoulder and asks.

"Did that ring the bell… Manish…" he asked and continued

"Did that remind you of something similar…" he asked again

Manish is quiet.

"Same modus operandi, same kind of threat, same Crypto Currency bank. Coincidence… I don't think so," says Professor Fabulous.

Mr. Rajput is clueless and is just standing quietly. Manish is still quiet. There is a strange and awkward silence in the room.

Manish takes off his glasses and fogs them using his breath from mouth and starts wiping them with his t-shirt. He wears his glasses and asks

"What do you want from me?"

"Manish… you have been a victim of a similar attack, I want you… to tell us the entire story in detail so that we can catch hold of this bastard…" says Professor Fabulous.

Manish takes a long breath and says

"As you know, after being deported from the United States, I lost all money, I lost all respect, my marriage was called off, my parents were ashamed of me and broke all ties with me, the only dream I had in my life had become the worst nightmare and cause of all misery and pain and I could not do anything about it. I was angry, dejected, it was the end of my life. But instead of hanging myself like a loser, I decided to take revenge.

I wanted the United States to pay for what they did to me. I started thinking of various ways of causing damage, I thought of hacking into White House and leaking intelligence to foreign countries which can destroy the US, I thought of going to Mexico and joining the drug mafia and send tons of drugs to the United States, I wanted United States to pay so bad that I even thought of joining ISIS" Manish pauses for a while and continues, both Professor Fabulous and Mr. Rajput are listening very carefully.

"But this was all pointless, I was nowhere capable of doing any of these I mentioned. But still, I wanted my revenge. I recollected my senses and gave a serious thought about it. I remembered one of our client's story, a middle-aged white woman who was scammed for $5000." Manish paused a few moments and continued looking at Professor Fabulous and asked.

"Do you remember Professor Saab... what I said about Americans..."

"Honest but not smart, kind but not cautious and no privacy..." Both Professor Fabulous and Manish answer at the same time and end with a little giggle.

"Absolutely correct..." says Manish

"And then the eureka happened. I will take my revenge on the United States by scamming Americans, I decided. I also knew from my stay in the United States that even if online scams were reported, they are of least priority to law enforcement agencies. They neither have budget nor resources to go behind an online scammer unless it was costing billions of dollars and somebody in authority will take serious note of it, which was highly unlikely. I recalled the entire story of the woman who was scammed for $5000. It was an IRS scam,"

"IRS??" said Mr. Rajput looking puzzled

"Internal Revenue Service (IRS) is basically the tax collection agency of the United States Government. It is one of the most powerful and feared agencies in the United States. Never mess with IRS is the first lesson thought to everyone in America." Says Manish and continues

"The modus operandi of the scam was very simple. Collect or buy details of phone numbers on the dark web. Many underground hackers sell this information."

"Dark web??" Mr. Rajput looking puzzled again

"Dark web… let's say if the internet is the main marketplace where everyone goes for all kinds of needs, Dark web is that small, dingy, dark alley which only a few people know and go to get drugs. Dark web sites contain anonymous message boards, online marketplaces for drugs, exchange for stolen financial and private data, child porn and any other illegal data," Manish explains

"Once you have the phone numbers and names from the dark web, search the person on social media like Facebook or for that matter just google the name. Most Facebook users have default privacy settings, which makes their profile visible to search engines. And then you know everything about them, their private life, professional life and if you go a little deeper,

who get access to their pictures and many other things." Manish pauses for a while and continues.

"Armed with all this information, you just need to make a phone call, pretending to be calling from the IRS. Tell the person that they have not paid their taxes or there is a fraud in their tax filing and an arrest warrant is issued and cops will be there anytime to arrest them. If they want to stop the arrest, they must pay $5000 immediately. Most of the Americans do not understand their taxes and always doubt if they have paid their taxes correctly. This unsureness accompanied with the details of their current or previous job or their house or any other information which is publicly available makes this call believable and that's why it works," Manish pauses for a few seconds before he could continue Mr. Rajput interjects and says

"Did you do the same thing…, I remember seeing a video on YouTube, where a scammer's computer network is destroyed by the person whom he had called…"

"No… I am not stupid to try an old scam that is already debunked, and people are aware of it. I rather turned my attention to social media. I thought of a new scam that was never heard. A long-distance military romance scam," Manish replies and continues.

"Military romance scam!!! What is that," asks Professor Fabulous

"During my stay in the United States, I noticed that in general there is a lot of respect for people serving in the US military, especially if you are a woman. I created a fake Facebook profile posing as a female military doctor who is stationed at

Los Angeles Air Force Base, El Segundo, California. I had also bought pictures of a real female military doctor from the dark web and posted them on Facebook and within no time I was getting flooded with friendship request," he replies.

"Modus operandi was simple. Pose as a female military doctor who is looking for her soulmate. Make online friendship with middle-aged white American men who are the easiest to scam. Show them some nice decent family pictures, share stories of high school dreams of serving country, show sadness and concern for soldiers and their families and finally ask for some financial help for a wounded soldier who is undergoing some treatment or for his family." Manish says.

"The scam was perfect. It had all the believable components in which Americans believe. Honor, pride, kindness, patriotism. It worked all the time. The only catch was it was slow. It took about three months to make the story completely believable. I made good money out of it. It went on for about a year with multiple different profiles. Then the scam was reported, and people became aware of it," Manish pauses.

Mr. Rajput is losing his patience but Professor Fabulous is listening to Manish carefully.

"Can you come straight to the point Manish... when and how did you encounter this cyber-attack," Mr. Rajput asks impatiently

"No... no... no... Mr. Rajput, not so soon. All good things to those who wait," he replies sarcastically.

"Anyway..." Manish continues from where he left

"After this scam and a few other similar scams, I hit the gold mine. It was Ashley Madison," says Manish

"Ashley Madison??? What is that," asks Mr. Rajput

"It is dating website, not for singles but married men and women. It is a place where you can have an affair. Life is short, have an affair, it says in its tag line," replies Manish

"What… A website for having an affair!!!" Mr. Rajput says with a surprise. He quickly opens the website on his iPad and shows it to Manish.

"Is this the one?" Mr. Rajput asks.

"Yes…" Manish replies

"Is this where you encountered the ransomware attack?" asks Mr. Rajput impatiently.

"No…" Manish replies

"Then… why you are enlightening us with all this bull shit… come straight to the point" Mr. Rajput says very seriously and looks very agitated, placing both hands on the table and leaning in towards Manish. Everyone is quiet for a few seconds; Manish looks at Professor Fabulous and says.

"It was not on Ashley Madison. But it was what I did to Mathew through this website made me see this day,"

"Mathew… who Mathew" Professor Fabulous asks Manish.

"Mathew Maguire was one of my targets on Ashley Madison. 32 years old, an innocent honest married family man from Berkley, California. He just happens to be browsing Ashley Madison for meeting someone over the long weekend when his wife and kid were away" Manish pauses for few seconds.

Mr. Rajput takes his iPad and starts doing something.

"Continue… What happened with Mathew Maguire?" asks Professor Fabulous. Manish is quiet, feeling uncomfortable to open about the incident. Professor Fabulous rephrases and asks again

"What did you do with Mathew Maguire and ended up here in jail?"

There is no answer from Manish. He is quiet. His eyes have gone red. His palms are sweating.

"Manish… this is your chance to help us and help yourself. You know very well that the United States is pushing very hard to extradite you and once you are in hands of FBI, you will die miserably." Professor Fabulous says seeing at Manish and continues

"If you help us in catching these attackers, I and Rajput both will testify and save you from the FBI. Isn't it? Rajput…" says Professor Fabulous nodding at Mr. Rajput for his reassurance.

"Sure… Sure Sir… Manish you have my word" Mr. Rajput replies still busy with his iPad.

"Tell me… what happened between you and Mathew Maguire" Professor Fabulous asks Manish again, but no answer. There is silence in the room and suddenly Mr. Rajput throws his iPad on the table and charges towards Manish. He grabs him by shirt placing his hands on his chest lifting him from the chair and pressing him against the wall and says in anger.

"You… killed him… you killed Mathew Maguire…"

Meanwhile, Professor Fabulous picks up the iPad and starts

reading a news report from the San Francisco Chronicle

"In a joint operation with the Indian Cyber Crime Division, FBI has arrested the online scammer in India who was behind multiple scams targeted towards Americans. Most recently this scammer was responsible for blackmailing and extorting money from UC Berkeley staffer Mathew Maguire, who was not able to bear the pressure and ended his life." Professor Fabulous pauses for a few seconds. Tears start rolling down from Manish's eyes. Professor Fabulous continues to read

"Mathew Maguire leaves behind his wife and a six-year-old son," Manish interrupts in between

"Stop… please stop…" he says while crying and sobbing. Mr. Rajput loosens his grips and frees Manish. Manish slowly slips down while crying profusely. Mr. Rajput and Professor Fabulous look at each other and give Manish a few minutes to vent out. After a few minutes, Professor Fabulous picks Manish up and makes him sit on the chair

"Relax… relax Manish…" he says and gives few more minutes to Manish to recollect himself.

"Hm… you were blackmailing Mathew to post his masturbating pictures on his Facebook page, which you obtained posing as an Indian woman on Ashley Madison, who wants to have an affair with white man," Mr. Rajput says

"But you must have done this to many other people before Mathew. Why did Mathew take such an extreme step?" asks Professor Fabulous.

"Unlike my previous military romance scam on Facebook, on Ashley Madison people did not come to find their soulmate.

They came to have an affair. People on Ashley Madison were very discreet and maintained a lot of secrecy. I tried various ways of scamming like paid sex chats, paid discreet meetup id batch or pay for online webcam show but nothing worked. Every time I talked about money; people stopped responding," Manish says.

"The only way to get money was to blackmail. The modus operandi was to pose as a sexually unsatisfied married Indian woman from San Francisco Bay Area seeking a one-night stand or weekend affair with white men. Getting their real identities was the key to this. Once I had their phone numbers and real names, it was a matter of a few minutes to know everything about them. Then record them masturbating on webcam and then blackmail them to post these pictures on their Facebook page or other social media platforms to get desired money. The more decent they were in their real-life more the money and less the time it took." Manish pauses and wipes his nose with his sleeves.

"What happened with Mathew…" asks Professor Fabulous

"Ahem…" Manish clears his throat and says

"Mathew was very naïve, he gave his real name, phone number, email, even his house address within a few minutes of chatting on Ashley Madison. He was a very decent family man in real life. It was just that his wife was so overwhelmed with a young kid, his school, his after school classes and house chores, that she had no time for sex and this sexual frustration led Mathew to Ashley Madison," he pauses for a few moments and continues.

"This is where I made a mistake, my overconfidence that

innocent honest family man will pay to maintain his secrecy went wrong," tears start rolling down again

"Instead of paying the money he ended his life..." his voice breaks as he speaks. It is clear to both Mr. Rajput and Professor Fabulous that he deeply regrets Mathew's death.

"What about the ransomware attack..." asks Mr. Rajput

Manish wipes his tears and says

"Mathew had stopped responding to my text messages, by the way, I never called anyone, I always texted them using a decoy United States phone number. I assumed that Mathew had decided not to pay, and I moved on with business as usual without knowing what had happened to Mathew,"

"Two weeks later... I was chatting with another person on Ashley Madison, the person sent me an attachment of his picture to my email. I thought I had found another target, the moment I opened the attachment, my laptop screen started flickering, the flickering became very heavy after a few seconds and it stopped at once. I was not understanding what was happening. Nothing was operational, the laptop had completely frozen. I was about to restart my laptop but suddenly the screen turned red and a message was displayed

'Mathew Maguire is no more, he committed suicide because of your stupid blackmail. You thought nobody can catch you. Today you are going to pay for your sins'"

Manish pauses for few seconds as Professor Fabulous and Mr. Rajput are listening very carefully

"Continue Manish..." says Mr. Rajput

"I was completely shocked, I was not at all understanding what was happening, I jumped out of my chair. I saw that the message disappeared, and pictures of Mathew's dead body started flashing on my screen along with his normal pictures with his wife and six-year-old son." Tears started rolling down again his cheeks, he sobbed and continued

"Suddenly a video appeared on screen, it was a kid, probably Mathew's six-year-old son. Where is daddy… Mama… where is daddy… the kid asked, holding his mother by her legs. I want daddy… the kid broke out crying loudly… I want daddy…I want daddy… I miss him so much…the kid continued crying," Manish says sobbing and crying profusely. Professor Fabulous and Mr. Rajput do not try to console him, they rather wait for few minutes so that Manish recollects himself. Manish wipes his nose with his sleeves and continues

"I was not understanding what to do… I was feeling very guilty… I was totally confused and shocked. I was just staring at the screen when my phone rang. It was an unknown number from the United States.

'Hello…' I said, with a shivering voice… there was no immediate answer

'Hello… hello…' I said again

'Answer the kid… maadrchod …' an agitated male voice replied

'Answer the kid… and tell him… that you killed his father… maadrchod…' the male voice said again

'Who are you…' I asked

'Chup…maadrchod… don't even dare to open your mouth

again...' he replied with a lot of anger

'I know you did all this for money... I can't bring back Mathew... but I will make sure that his kid will not be deprived of the future he deserved,' he said while I was listening quietly.

'I will take away... all your money and you will rot to death in jail... Maadrchod...' he said and disconnected the call.

Soon after the call got disconnected, I started getting multiple messages from banks. Balance in all my bank accounts had fallen below the minimum value. Until then I had about twenty-seven crore rupees in different bank accounts. All of that money was transferred to a bank in Estonia to some Cryptocurrency Bank" Manish pauses for few moments and continues.

"Before I could understand anything, police charged suddenly in my house, breaking down the main door. And arrested me and bought me here. I later came to know that the person who called me not only took all my money but had tipped FBI and Indian Cyber Cell of my location with all the evidence."

"Until today... I cannot forget the face of the kid, I cannot sleep, because the moment I close my eyes, I hear Mathew's son helpless cries." Manish puts his facedown weeping.

Mr. Rajput places his hand on Manish's shoulder firmly and consoles him. After a few moments, Professor Fabulous looks at Manish and says

"Revenge is contagious Manish... you got so blinded by feeling of vengeance that you killed an innocent man who had nothing to do with you being deported from the USA. You took your revenge and so did the other person for Mathew's death," he pauses and gets up from his chair and continues

"And maybe this is the same person who is now taking revenge on everyone for sharing and spreading fake news," He pauses again and walks few steps away from the table.

"What do you think Manish, who could have done this to you? Mathew cannot because he was dead by this time. Someone from India who must have been close to Mathew's family because he mentioned about Mathew's child. Can you recall anything Mathew could have told you, anything about Indian friend or colleague," he asks Manish.

"Hm… nothing… Mathew did not mention anyone like that," Manish replies.

"Hm… ok…" he says and grabs his phone from the table and looks at Mr. Rajput indicating him that it is time to leave, Mr. Rajput grabs his iPad and few other papers which he had dropped on the floor.

"Ok… Manish… you take care…, if we catch the culprits behind today's attack based on your information, I will try my best to stop your extradition to the United States," he says and walks towards the door and Mr. Rajput follows him, while Manish is still seated on the chair.

"One last thing Manish…" Professor Fabulous says before exiting

"Your remorse is very much visible; you deeply regret what you did. But repentance is only half of your *prayaashchit* (atonement). It will be completed if Mathew's wife and especially his six-year-old son forgives you. This jail is only a material punishment." Professor Fabulous and Mr. Rajput leave the room.

While walking outside, Mr. Rajput feels that even though what Professor said about repentance and forgiveness was for Manish, but he is indirectly referring to himself, he is guilty and repenting from within. But knowing Professor Fabulous, he understands very well that Professor will never confess it. He will keep making indirect references that he is remorse full and sorry for what he did four years ago. But his ego will not allow him to say sorry.

Chapter 7

THE UNKNOWN INDIAN YOUTH

Outside the Central Jail, Professor Fabulous and Mr. Rajput are walking towards Mr. Rajput's car.

"What now Professor…" asks Mr. Rajput

"We need to find out more about Mathew Maguire… It is obvious that it is an Indian man, who had called Manish. Someone close to Mathew's child" says Professor Fabulous

"Berkeley is a university town; I am familiar with it. Many Indian students studying at UC Berkeley do odd jobs to earn some pocket money. Babysitting, working in restaurants or providing tuitions to school kids are popular options. I think…" before Professor could continue further, Mr. Rajput gets a phone call. It is from Mr. Magadi, his boss.

"Sorry Sir… I have to take this…" says Mr. Rajput holding his smartphone. Professor Fabulous just nods

"Sir…" says Mr. Rajput

"Ok… ok… right now???"

"Ok… Yes… Sir… he is with me… I will bring him along…"

says Mr. Rajput and disconnects the call.

"Sir… we have to go to headquarters right now…" says Mr. Rajput looking at Professor Fabulous. Professor Fabulous lifts his shoulder in a half shrug and opens his arms questioning Mr. Rajput.

"Mr. Natarajan, Facebook India head, has just now received an email. It has a video message. A rogue hacking group has claimed responsibility for this attack and is demanding $500 million. He needs our help to find the origin of the email. Mr. Magadi needs me to be there, he has told me to bring you along…" Mr. Rajput replies.

Professor Fabulous looks at his watch for the time then looks at Mr. Rajput and thinks for a few moments and says

"Waste of time…"

"You go ahead Rajput… I want to find out more about Mathew Maguire," says Professor Fabulous

"Sir… you have come across many rogue hackers and cyber-criminal gangs… your expi…" before Mr. Rajput could complete, Professor Fabulous interjects and says

"That's why… that's why Rajput… I am telling you it is a waste of time… it is not any rogue hacker…"

"Sir… but we have to look at all possibilities, last time I didn't do my due diligence and followed you blindly and we both know what happened…" replies Mr. Rajput

Professor Fabulous gets in the car without saying anything. Even though he disagrees with Mr. Rajput, he understands that he has done his fair share of mistakes in the past to which

Mr. Rajput is not only a witness but a victim too. Rajput also gets in the car and instructs his driver to drive to headquarters.

Mr. Rajput gets busy making a few phone calls to his subordinates, while Professor Fabulous grabs Mr. Rajput's iPad and starts looking for any information about Mathew Maguire. In normal circumstances he could have just done a simple google search with Mathew Maguire's name and the first link to appear will be the Facebook page and few more specific searches on Facebook, he could have all the information he needs. But since Facebook is down, he first goes on the UC Berkeley website to check if any information is still available on Mathew Maguire. Being a professor, he knew that universities no matter where, do a very sloppy job in keeping their website up to date. If he is not wrong, he will be able to find Mathew's profile on UC Berkeley's staff directory and as expected Mathew's profile still existed even after his death. Mathew was a librarian at UC Berkeley, that's why the news report stated him as staffer instead of calling him academic or Professor. There was a nice headshot of Mathew. Apart from that, he could not find anything more.

After going through a few more news report which stated same things, he came across one news report which had a picture of Mathew's wife, which probably was taken when she was talking to a local news channel about the incident. In the picture, Professor Fabulous sees a young Indian man, standing behind Mathew's wife holding Mathew's son in his arms.

"This… face… I have seen this boy somewhere…" Professor Fabulous says to himself.

Professor Fabulous zooms in the picture and focuses only on the face of an Indian boy.

"Where…. where… I have seen this boy…" he is trying to recall.

Mr. Rajput completes his phone call. He sees Professor Fabulous in deep thought

"What happened Professor…" he asks

"Hm… sorry, what?" Professor replies

"What happened, what are you looking at," Mr. Rajput asks again.

Professor Fabulous zooms out of the picture and gives him the iPad and says

"Look at this picture, it is Mathew's wife…" He pauses for a few seconds while Mr. Rajput takes a look.

"What about her…" Mr. Rajput asks

"Look at the man standing behind her, an Indian boy…" Mr. Rajput zooms in the picture and says

"I see him… what about him…" he asks

"I have met him somewhere… I can't remember where… but I have met him." Professor Fabulous replies.

 The car stops at a traffic red signal. Professor Fabulous gazes outside the car window trying hard to recall the boy in the picture and where he had seen him. Suddenly out of nowhere, a flying drone crashes on Mr. Rajput's window.

"Wow!!!" exclaims Professor Fabulous in shock and jumps slightly on his seat. Mr. Rajput doesn't react. The driver continues to drive seeing the green light. As the car proceeds further, Professor sees a street vendor standing right below the traffic light and selling cheap duplicate drones. He is flying one of these drones to the windows of cars standing in the traffic and attracting attention to his business.

"Anything is possible in India…" Professor Fabulous says to himself and then suddenly, just like a strike of lightning, he remembers where he had seen the boy in the picture. The flying drone had triggered a relative memory string in his brain and helped him to recall that he had seen the boy a few years back in San Francisco in a conference on Artificial Intelligence and Machine learning.

The dancing robotic dog from Boston Dynamics Inc received maximum attention in the conference and while Professor was watching the demo of the same, A military drone, which was getting showcased by a startup company, had come crashing down on him. If it was not for this boy in the picture, Professor could have ended up in the hospital. The boy in the picture had pushed him in the right time and saved him from the drone.

He also remembers that he was supposed to share the stage for a panel discussion with Dr. Mary Aiken, a renowned Forensic Cyber psychologist, but he had walked into another room accidentally and as soon as he entered, the audience had clapped, but it was not for him, it was for the person on the stage. The room was dark, he could hardly see anything but a screen which displayed the topic of the talk "Fake news: I have a solution". As he was about to leave, he saw the same boy who had saved him from the drone on the stage.

"Sir…" Mr. Rajput says but Professor doesn't respond.

"Professor… are you ok…" says Mr. Rajput seeing him

motionless. He puts his hand on Professor's back and gives a gentle shake

"Sir… what happened…"

"Hm…" Professor shrugs in shock at once.

"I remember… I remember now…" he says and continues

"I had seen him in San Francisco, at a conference. He presented something about Fake news…"

"Do you remember his name?" asks Mr. Rajput

"No… not name, but he was a student of UC Berkeley…" Professor replies

"Search on YouTube, 'Fake news: I have a solution', This was the topic of his talk, I am sure somebody could have recorded it and uploaded to YouTube," says Professor Fabulous to Mr. Rajput

As directed, Mr. Rajput starts searching on YouTube for the topic mentioned by Professor. After going through multiple videos on fake news, finally, on the fourth page, he sees a video having the title "AI conference: Fake news". The thumbnail shows the picture of the same Indian boy.

"Sir… is this the one…" Mr. Rajput asks Professor holding the iPad in front of him.

"Play it…" Professor replies

Mr. Rajput plays the video, turns the volume high and makes it full screen. Both Professor Fabulous and Mr. Rajput lean forward from their seats to see. The video starts with applause from the audience, this is where Professor Fabulous had accidentally entered the room. The presenter is the same Indian youth dressed in a sky-blue cotton shirt which is neatly tucked in black pants. A thick dense head full of hair that is parted in the middle. He is about 5 feet 11 inches. Fair complexion, rounded nose with eyebrows meeting in the middle of a square forehead. Clean shaved. With a heavy Indian accent, he says

"Snapchat is going to shut down by the end of this year". There are some giggles and chuckles in the audience.

"Let me say that one more time… Snapchat the social media app that we used to share photos and pictures, that is going to shut down by the end of this year" he said again. There were awe and shock in the audience. Audience murmurs phrases like

"Aw…. that so sad…." "What… seriously…" "He is kidding…" and so on.

The presenter allowed the audience to express their shock and after a few moments, he said

"This… my friends… is an example of fake news…"

"You may giggle, you may chuckle and laugh but this was a reality for many users a few days ago on twitter. A piece of fake news came out that said Snapchat was going to shut down by end of this year," He shows the screenshots of twitter feed of this fake news and says.

"And the most strange and absurd thing happened… many people start picking this fake news and start talking that how sad and unfortunate it was and the service which they love so much, it is going to shut down by end of this year," He pauses for few moments

"However, this was Fake news, and this story got so big, that Snapchat itself had to come out and make an official press release that they are not shutting down," He pauses and continues

"Let us think about this for a second. Snapchat is a multi-billion-dollar company listed on the New York Stock exchange, yet a piece of fake news was so powerful that they have to come out to deny it…" He pauses

"Plato has said many wise things, and one of the things he has said was to decide the meaning of the words before starting any discussion. Therefore, before going into more details of the rise of Fake news, I want to decide on the meaning of word Fake news."He pauses and continues,

"Let us see what the meaning of word fake news is. To be honest, I was unable to find a dictionary definition of this term, but the closest and simplest meaning of fake news is…" he pauses and displays the definition and reads

"false information which appears to be true" he says and waits for few moments so that audience can grasp the definition.

"Further the term 'information' in this definition can be classified as misinformation which is inadvertent sharing of false information and disinformation which is creation and sharing of information known to be already false with malice intent" he explains.

"But the issue of fake news is not new. It always existed. But in the last decade the marriage of a smartphone with social media has accelerated and amplified the fake news," he says.

"And now it has come to the extent, that we as a society are unable to tell the difference between fact and an opinion. For example," he pauses for a few moments and pointing to his shirt says

"The color of this shirt is blue…that is a fact, and nobody can dispute that," he pauses and continues

"The color of this shirt is awesome!!! That is an opinion… it is highly subjective, biased and customized to individual needs." the audience chuckles

"The color of this shirt gives me superpowers… that is false or fake news…" the audience giggles

"What has happened today, as we are bombarded with huge unvetted news or information…we have forgotten to distinguish all these terms I mentioned. We all have fallen prey to conformational bias… which is nothing but sharing the information which confirms our beliefs, it does not matter if it is true or false. As long as it says what we already believe in, we are all okay with it," says the presenter.

Both Mr. Rajput and Professor Fabulous are watching the video very attentively when an annoying unskippable five-second ad interjects the video

 "His thoughts are very mature considering his age… isn't it? Rajput…" says Professor Fabulous. The ad completes, and the video continues

"Fake news is like climate change, you can ignore it, but it will not ignore you."

"Fake news is very real which has and will have many dangerous consequences. A piece of fake news caused massive riots between Hindus and Muslims in Sri Lanka. Two youths were assumed to be child kidnappers in India and were lynched and murdered due to a piece of fake news. And not to forget the unprecedented civil unrest and social tension fake news has caused all around the globe. These are only a few examples…" the presenter pauses for a few seconds.

"But… I am not here to crib or whine about fake news. As the title of my talk says, I am here to offer a solution," he says.

"If technology has created this problem, I can use the same technology to get rid of this problem… But I am not the first one to have this idea…"

"There are many sincere and similar efforts been made. Even before the advent of social media, a website named hoaxslayer.com, which is still active has always debunked fake news and conspiracy theories…"

"In recent times, many small companies offered a solution… like… this app…" he shows on the screen.

"It charges you to check if news article shared on Facebook is real or fake… The first time I came to know about this… I was like seriously … I have to pay every time to make sure the news is not fake…" the audience giggles.

"That's not going to happen… whoever thought of this… it is a lame business idea…"

"Here is another one… this app is free; it can tell you whether the picture posted on any social media platform is fake or real. But it is full of ads, it takes tons of time and most of the time it is wrong…" the audience laughs

"Then there are these intellectuals… advising us to become fact-checkers… and to do our own research before sharing anything on social media and to stop using social media and to go back to basics and believe in only traditional media… which by the way is more biased than social media," the presenter says in a single breath.

"God… seriously… give me a break…" the presenter exclaims.

Both Professor Fabulous and Mr. Rajput smile while watching and listening to the video very carefully.

"But let us face it, fake news is not going anywhere, social media is here to stay. We all are a bunch of lazy clickers, we read only headlines, we don't have time for fact-checking and no way… we want to pay for fact-checking and honestly, nobody cares until it affects them…" he pauses for a few moments.

"Keeping all this in mind… I and my friends at UC Berkeley have developed this technology using Artificial Intelligence and advance machine learning algorithms." He pauses for a few seconds

"It comes as an add-on plugin compatible with all social media platforms. It will detect and label fake news before you can share it, in real-time. It keeps running in the background, consumes almost no battery and boy… it is free…" the audience giggles.

The video stops. Both Professor Fabulous and Mr. Rajput look at each other at the same time. They both move back in their seats.

Mr. Rajput says holding the iPad in his hand

"The video was published about a year ago. It has 39576 views till now. The channel name is counter_fakenews. This is the only video on the channel. No mention of any name of the presenter, there are no comments on the video…"

"We still don't know who this youth is…"

"Can you remember anything else about the conference Professor…" asks Mr. Rajput

Professor Fabulous takes the iPad in his hand and tries to remember. He recalls that he had met the boy later that day at dinner. He had walked up to him and shook his hand to thank him for saving him from the crashing drone.

"Thank you… Thank you… for saving me from the drone… oh boy… that was scary…" Professor recalls saying to the boy.

"Oh…that one… don't worry about it…" he had replied very casually.

"I had accidentally walked in during your talk… but I had to be part of another panel discussion at the same time and could not listen to you. I am interested to know more about your solution for fake news." He recalls saying to him and remembers that the young Indian boy showed him a demo of his technology.

"Sir…Professor…Can you remember anything else…" asks Mr. Rajput once again.

"Yes…Yes… I had met him later that day, for thanking him for saving me from the drone…" Professor replies

"He also showed the demo of his technology…it was very impressive, it detected fake news on social media platforms in real-time and labeled them before users could share it," he says

"Did you ask his name…" asks Mr. Rajput

Professor Fabulous shakes his head signaling no.

"Oh God…Professor your arrogance!!!…" exclaims Mr. Rajput

"Arre…Yaar… he didn't ask my name, nor I asked his name. Neither I introduced myself nor he introduced. Where does arrogance come in the picture here…" Professor Fabulous says

"You didn't ask his name because you felt it is not important, you feel only your opinion matters, only your name matters… you were the same then and you are the same now. Overconfident arrogant selfish!!!" Mr. Rajput yells in frustration. The car stops at the main gate of the National Cyber Defense headquarters for a security check. The security guards confirm the identity of Mr. Rajput and the car is allowed to pass. Professor Fabulous doesn't react to Rajput's comments. He is quiet but feeling a little happy that at least Mr. Rajput is loosening up a little.

Chapter 8

ANONYMOUS

The new government takes cybersecurity very seriously and has spent about Rs.400 crores of money in upgrading technology. As part of this upgrade, National Cyber Defense has a new building.

The campus is secured by a large wall of around 8 feet tall with only one entry and exit point which is secured by military guards 24 Hours. It is a three-floor building, the exterior walls are made of Flexi glass just like a modern software company. The car drops Professor Fabulous and Mr. Rajput in front of the main entrance which is again secured by military guards. Professor Fabulous is asked to leave his phone at the security checkpoint. Professor looks at Mr. Rajput to see if he intervenes

"Security Protocol sir… I hope you understand…" says Mr. Rajput,

Professor unwillingly hands over his phone to security. They walk through the main hallway and enter another section of the building where a few people are working, each one of them having multiple monitors on their desk. Standing at a corner Mr. Rajput calls

"Shirke…" an officer who is busy watching some CCTV footage. BF Magadi, the chief who runs this place, has a unique recruiting policy. Each recruit can bring one confidant with them to join the cyber defense, of course, they must go through all the necessary screening but in this way, he has completely trustworthy people. Srikant Shirke was and is the confidant of Mr. Rajput. He is also familiar with Professor Fabulous. Shirke stops video which is playing on his monitor and walks up to Mr. Rajput and says

"Sir…" at the same time he sees Professor Fabulous and says

"Arre… Professor Fabulous…I was just guessing this morning after the attack that Rajput sir will surely get you on this… it is good to see you…"

Professor Fabulous is just listening quietly pretending to recognize him, but he is very bad in remembering people.

"Shirke take a look at this YouTube video," Mr. Rajput quickly plays the same video on his iPad which he and Professor Fabulous were watching in the car. He hands over the iPad to Shirke and says

"Professor strongly believes that this is the person behind the attack. But we don't know his identity." He pauses while Shirke is watching the video

"Take some snapshots and search in all the government databases. Passport, Aadhar card, pan card, voter id, bhriver's license anything which matches this face… I want all the information on this person…" he says

"Sir… I will search all the databases and find out…" Shirke replies and goes back to his desk with Mr. Rajput's iPad in hand

"Very impressive... I was thinking that you spent all the money only on the building... but looks like things have gotten more serious this time" says Professor Fabulous looking at the overall technology upgrade in the facility.

"Sir... let us see what Mr. Natarajan has for us... this way sir..." says Mr. Rajput and takes Professor Fabulous towards the elevator and they both get in. After a few seconds the elevator door opens, they are not on the 2nd or 3rd floor, but four floors down. As soon as the elevator door opens, Professor sees a large underground military bunker with rows of high speed, high-performance military-grade computer servers, large monitors and other military-grade equipment.

"The engine of the train is here...where all the real work happens..." says Mr. Rajput looking at Professor Fabulous

"hm...Sherlock Holmes... is becoming James Bond... but the sexy women are still missing..." replies Professor Fabulous jokingly and gives one more try to see if Mr. Rajput reacts but still stone-cold plain face. Professor Fabulous misses the camaraderie he shared in the past with Mr. Rajput.

They both walk in a small room with only a round table and a flat sixty-five inch monitor mounted on the wall. Mr. Natarajan and BF Magadi are already present in the room. On the table is a laptop of Mr. Natarajan connected to sixty-five inch monitor and an intercom speakerphone. As soon as Mr. Rajput and Professor Fabulous enter the room, Mr. Magadi presses a button on the intercom telephone. The telephone goes automatically in speaker mode and after two rings

"Sir..." says a female voice

"What happened to Mr. Natarajan's email trace... have we

found the origin" asks Mr. Magadi

"Sir… our initial trace is pointing to multiple locations. Ukraine…Syria…Malaysia… but we will have the final trace very soon sir…" replies female voice

"Hurry up…" says Mr. Magadi and disconnects the call.

"Sir…" Mr. Rajput greets BF Magadi

"This is Professor Fabulous… expert of Forensic Cyber Psychology…" Professor Fabulous extends his hand while Mr. Rajput introduces him.

"This is Retired Air Wing Commander and Chief of National Cyber Defense BF Magadi," Mr. Rajput says pointing his hand at Mr. Magadi

"And Mr. Natarajan Facebook India head" pointing at Mr. Natarajan. All three of them shake hands.

"Forensic Cyber Psychology…what is that???" asks Mr. Natarajan looking at Professor Fabulous

"In short it is the study of changing human behavior due to technology created by people like you…" Professor Fabulous replies sarcastically.

"Anyway, …we don't have time… show us what you have" says Professor Fabulous.

"Here Professor…" Mr. Magadi points to the monitor where the video sent to Mr. Natarajan starts playing. The video starts with the famous V for Vendetta mask or the Guy Fawkes mask, named for a seventeenth-century Briton who infamously attempted to bomb the House of Lords. He was planning to assassinate King James 1 so that his Catholic daughter could ascend to the throne. A stylized portrayal of a face with a smile and red cheeks, a wide mustache upturned at both ends, and a thin vertical pointed beard, designed by illustrator David Lloyd. After appearing in Web forums, the mask became a well-known symbol for the online hacktivist group Anonymous and other anti-government, anti-establishment protests around the world. This has led to the popular name Anonymous mask.

The video starts slowly zooming out and a distorted male voice can be heard

"We are Anonymous…We are Legion…We do not forgive; we do not forget …Expect us…"

The voice repeats while the video keeps zooming out

"We are Anonymous…We are Legion…We do not forgive; we do not forget …Expect us…"

In the video, A man wearing a V for Vendetta mask and a black hoody appears on the screen. Only his upper body is visible, it appears as though he is seated. He is holding a few papers with both of his hands. Towards the right of the man there is an emblem. The emblem shows a headless man wearing a black suit and tie with both hands folded to his back and located in the middle of two branches of fig leaves. In the position of the head, a question mark is placed. The hooded man starts reading from the paper in the same distorted male voice and says

"Citizens of the world… as we had promised… we have bought down the tyrant…"

"We had warned you… We had warned you to stop invading

our privacy … we had warned you to not impose your policies on us…we had warned you not to treat us like a commodity which you can use for your selfish benefits…" the distorted male voice says

"But… you did not listen… you continued to destroy our privacy, you continued to sell our emotions for your corrupt ambition…"

"In the name of your policy and business strategy you kept eroding our rights…"

"But today…it stops…"

"Your intellectually incompetent overpaid engineering force will not be able to get rid of us…"

"And if you are not able to resolve this matter by this evening, the next day morning in the United States you are finished, your stock, your reputation everything is gone…"

"But… we give you one last chance, to save yourself the humiliation…"

"Pay us $500 million and we will terminate the attack. Else it will continue to spread across the world"

"We are Anonymous…We are Legion…We do not forgive; we do not forget …Expect us…" the distorted male voice says and the video ends.

There is silence for a few minutes in the room. Professor Fabulous looks at Mr. Rajput and then at Mr. Natarajan and says

"Seriously…Natarajan…you called us here to show this…"

says Professor Fabulous in an agitated voice

"Isn't it obvious that Anonymous is behind this…" Mr. Natarajan replies

"What is obvious to me is that… just like the users of Facebook, you have given up all reasoning…" says Professor Fabulous

"Why Professor…why it can't be Anonymous… they are a rogue hacking group, they are known for their notorious methods of hacking, they are spread across the globe, they had disappeared for few years… and this may be their big come back…" says Mr.Natarajan without taking any offense for Professor's insulting comments.

"I am with Natarajan here…" Mr. Magadi seconds Mr. Natarajan's thoughts.

"If you guys could have known little more about Anonymous and seen the video carefully … we would not be wasting time discussing this…" Professor Fabulous says

"Please…enlighten us… we are dumb assholes…" says Mr. Natarajan who looks a little irritated

Professor Fabulous looking at Mr. Magadi and Mr. Rajput says

"Anonymous…never claims responsibility for anything they have done, in an email to individual…"

"They claim responsibility in full public domain… either by posting a video on YouTube or social media or on the website they hacked… take any of their attacks, either attack on Scientology in the United States, or ISIS and ISIS sympathizers websites…" Professor Fabulous pauses and continues

"Whatever Anonymous has done till now, right or wrong, the public sentiment has always been with them. Anonymous never demands money and if they do... they lose all public support and a hacktivist group can never survive without public being on their side." Professor Fabulous pauses and continues

"And finally, Anonymous can never do this kind of attack which undermines free speech. They are against censorship; that was one of the main reasons why Anonymous came to existence. If they do this ... then their whole existence is nullified. They will not be a hacktivist group... but like you said, they will be recognized as a bunch of rogue hackers doing illegal activities for personal gain..." Professor Fabulous looks at Mr.Natarajan and Mr.Magadi who are listening to him very attentively, but they still are not looking completely convinced.

"Furthermore...if you observe the video carefully and compare it to other videos of Anonymous, you can easily deduce that the video is not from Anonymous." He pauses and continues

"For example, the emblem is on the right in this video...whereas it is always on the left if you see past videos of Anonymous. The body language of the hooded man is completely out of sync. His hand gestures, his head movement never match with what he is saying. This is not Anonymous..." says Professor Fabulous. After a few moments of silence.

"Who else can do this..." Mr. Natarajan asks but does not wait for an answer and continues

"An attack of this massive scale can only be done with many hackers working in collaboration with each other and you know very well only Anonymous has this ability to gather hackers across the globe for their rogue activities…" says Mr. Natarajan

"Wait…wait…wait…" Mr. Rajput intervenes

"In the video, he demanded $500 million, but didn't tell how or where to send this money…" says Mr. Rajput who was quiet all this time, looking at Mr. Natarajan

"No… he did tell that…but not in the video but the email…" Mr. Natarajan quickly opens the email sent to him and displays it on the monitor which has only one single sentence. He reads the email aloud

"$500 million, in cryptocurrency, to the account number 007511156375890 CRYPTO CODE: SSWIB0045617

Pay using www.worldcryptobank.com"

"What do you have to say now, Professor…same account number, same CRYPTO code…same Crypto Currency Bank…" asks Mr. Natarajan but without waiting for an answer he continues

"Why would someone not responsible for today's attack want the money in the same account and same bank…isn't it foolish…"

"It is not rocket science, it is just common sense…simple common sense, which so-called intellectuals and academics like you are missing today…" Mr. Natarajan says sarcastically to Professor Fabulous, in reply to his previous mean comments. But Professor Fabulous is busy in reading the email sent to Mr. Natarajan…he has moved a step forward towards the monitor, the email reads

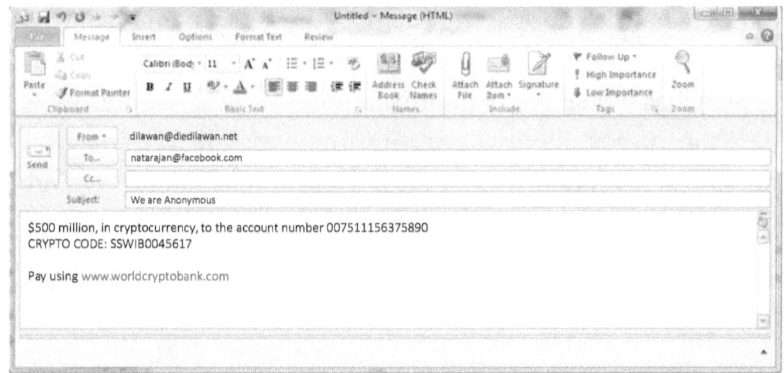

"What is it Professor…" asks Mr. Rajput

"hm… this word … 'dilawan'… I was wondering if any of you are aware of this word 'dilawan'" Professor replies, pauses for a second, looks at Mr. Natarajan and continues

"You…Mr.Natarajan…you must be very familiar with this word, it gets used very often by people who spend the highest time on social media in the world…and I am sure because of this single word your company makes billions of dollars…"

"Dila…wan… Indians never use this word. I have never heard of it…and who other than Indians spend maximum time on social media…" replies Mr. Natarajan

"You are so misinformed and arrogant… just like users of your platform…" Professor takes another mean jibe at Mr. Natarajan

"What is this word 'dilawan' Professor…" asks Mr. Rajput as the tension between Professor Fabulous and Mr. Natarajan is clearly visible

"It is the Filipinos, the citizens or I should say netizens of the Philippines who spend about ten hours a day on social media, the highest in the world… not Indians" Professor replies

"And what is happening across the world the same is happening in the Philippines… the rise of extreme right-wing … which is efficiently exploiting social media… to spread age-old conspiracy theories…misinformation…disinformation… fake news to manipulate people's mind" Professor says and pauses for few moments and continues

"Like in India… anyone who disagrees with government or supports the party in opposition or anyone opposes government policies is conveniently termed as Anti-National or Traitor by social media users. Similarly, Filipinos use the word 'Dilawan' which means 'yellowed', to dismiss and silence anyone supporting the Liberal Party." Professor pauses for a few moments and continues

"As more people are getting access to the internet and social media in developing nations like the Philippines, cybercrime has also risen proportionally. In the last few years due to slowing economy Philippines has seen a sudden rise in cyber gangs who usually target US nationals" Professor pauses and looks at Mr. Natarajan and says

"It must be one of the cyber gangs in the Philippines who could have sent this email and trying to extort money, taking advantage of the situation"

"But…Profes…" before Mr. Natarajan could complete, the intercom phone rings, everyone goes silent as Mr. Magadi answers the call

"Sir…" Says the same female voice as before when Mr. Magadi had called to check the status of email trace

"What is it…" asks Mr. Magadi

"Sir…we have completed the trace… the email was sent from Manila, Philippines using internet connection registered on name Rudy Paule…" the female voice replies with some excitement

There is silence in the room for a few seconds, everyone in the room is looking at Professor Fabulous.

"Ok… get me the complete log…" Mr. Magadi says and disconnects the call. He looks at Mr. Rajput and asks

"Rajput…what is your status…"

"Sir…Professor Fabulous has narrowed down an individual of interest. An Indian student studying at UC Berkeley. We have his picture but no identity yet. Shirke is looking in the government databases to get a match…and we are pretty sure that either he is behind this attack or he knows who is behind this attack…" Mr. Rajput replies

"This cannot be one person's job… and definitely not a student… this kind of attack can only be done by this rogue criminal cyber gang Anonymous or whoever is pretending to be Anonymous…" Mr. Natarajan says disagreeing with Mr.Rajput.

"I have told you before Anonymous is not a criminal cyber gang, they are a hacktivist group…" Professor Fabulous reacts to Mr. Natarajan.

"Are you a terrorist sympathizer Professor… like all other intellectuals of our country…" asks Mr. Magadi without any hesitation.

"I am not sympathizing with anyone and this is not terrorist attack" Professor replies

"This is no less than a terrorist attack…" Mr. Natarajan replies immediately.

"Then what were you doing all this time Natarajan… weren't you knowing that from day one… your social media platform is spreading fake news and you have been giving lame excuses that you are not responsible for what people say on your platform…" Professor Fabulous counters Mr.Natarajan's argument in a single breath and pauses for a few moments. He looks at Mr. Natarajan straight in the eyes and says

"What has happened today is just an extreme outburst of frustration as a reaction for your unwillingness to do nothing to curb fake news"

This tense atmosphere of the room is interrupted by another call on the intercom phone. After two rings Mr. Magadi answers the call, it is officer Srikanth Shirke to whom Mr. Rajput had given the job of identifying the unknown Indian youth using his pictures from the YouTube video.

"Sir Shirke…" he says

"What is it Shirke?" asks Mr. Magadi

"Sir… we have the match…it is the same person whom Rajput Sir showed me on the video…" Shirke replies

"What video?" asks Mr. Magadi

"Sir…Professor Fabulous had met a student from UC Berkeley a few years ago at a conference. He is the person of interest in this case, he had demonstrated his software by which fake news can be identified. I was able to find his talk on YouTube. Shirke referred the same video to extract some pictures and compare them with the government databases." Mr. Rajput clarifies.

"Rajput will be there in a second…" Mr. Magadi says and disconnects the call.

"Professor…" Mr. Magadi says and by placing his hand on Mr. Rajput's back he continues

"Rajput… somehow believes that you are the person who can save us from this crisis. Even though I always had reservations for academics and intellectuals, I am willing to bet this time because Rajput trust's you and I trust Rajput." Mr. Magadi says, pauses for a few moments and continues

"You better get going now… meanwhile, I will take care of this Philippines cyber gang and find out if there is any truth to this threat"

Mr. Rajput and Professor Fabulous leave the room and head towards the elevator. In the elevator, Professor asks Mr. Rajput

"So… you still trust me…" Mr. Rajput looks at Professor with a sense of irritation

"That's what Mr. Magadi said… that you trust me…" Professor rephrases

"I said, I trust your work…" Mr. Rajput replies with little anger on his face. Before Professor could say anything, the elevator door opens, Mr. Rajput walks out. Professor Fabulous follows him to Shirke's desk.

Chapter 9

MELTDOWN

"Shirke…show us what do you have," says Mr. Rajput. Mr. Shirke instead of standing up just turns around his chair facing Mr. Rajput and Professor Fabulous, holding his wireless keyboard in his hands.

"Sir… I scanned all the government records and found about 13,000 matching facial profile to the person of interest. These matches include Aadhar cards, pan cards, Driver's License, Passports issued from various cities in India." Mr. Shirke replies and presses a few keys on his keyboard. Two out of three monitors on his desk, the left and the right to be specific start displaying the matches he had found and the monitor in the middle is displaying different facial snapshots of the person of interest which Mr.Shirke had captured from the YouTube video.

"But… from the video it is evident that the person of interest is a student at UC Berkeley, California, USA…" Mr. Shirke says

"That's why I narrowed my search to passport matches only…" He presses another key on the keyboard and only passport matches start displaying on the left and right monitors.

"Out of 13,000 matching records, there were about 600 matching passports. And out of these 600 passports only 56 had traveled outside India…" he pauses and continues

"Further detailed search on these 56 passports revealed that only 21 of them had traveled to the United States and only 1 of these 21 traveled on a Student VISA…" he pauses and presses another key on his keyboard. The left and the right monitors start displaying the passport which is matching to the picture in the middle monitor.

"And this is your guy!!!" he says and stands up from his chair, throwing his keyboard on the desk. Mr. Rajput and Professor Fabulous both look at each other and then start looking at the monitors very carefully. It is the same Indian student whom Professor had met and is in the YouTube video. Mr. Rajput looks at Professor Fabulous for his confirmation, Professor nods his head to confirm that the match is correct. The address on the passport is of Pune, India.

"Good Job Shirke… Rajput has trained you well" compliments Professor Fabulous looking at Mr. Rajput as though the compliment was for him not for Mr. Shirke.

"Anything else Shirke… we should know…" asks Mr. Rajput ignoring Professor Fabulous's compliment

"Yes Sir…I found matching Aadhar card and Driver License with the same name and same address as it is on the passport" Mr. Shirke replies

"Same address on Passport, Driver's License and Aadhar card, that means he is native of the same place and stays in the same address probably with his parents," says Mr. Rajput

"Also, sir… the very important thing, immigration record indicates that he came to India about a year ago and then didn't leave the country…" Mr. Shirke says

"hm… very good Shirke…" Professor Fabulous compliments Mr. Shirke once again and asks

"Any mobile phone number or internet connection registered on this name and address…"

"Sir… we found one postpaid number registered on the same name and address and it is still active, we tried calling the number, but no one is answering" replies Mr. Shirke

"Get the complete call records…past six months or more…" says Mr. Rajput

"Yes…Sir…" Mr. Shirke replies

"What are we waiting for Rajput … let's go … we have to get to Pune…" Professor says

"Sir… before you leave one last thing. Somebody tried a 'clean slate' and they were largely successful but could not infiltrate government database." Mr. Shirke says looking at Mr. Rajput

"Clean Slate? what is that Rajput???" asks Professor Fabulous

"Sir… there are different ways these days, both legal and illegal to wipe out anything and everything on the internet about a person, this includes any reviews or news articles, or comments made on social media. There are legal companies that help celebrities or business owners or any other person to clean their online image by deleting any negative reviews or comments about them. Once 'clean slate' is executed the online information about a person is deleted but it leaves a footprint which shows up in diagnostics" explains Mr. Rajput

"Hm…ok… it is obvious that this person does not want to be found… let us go now…"

"Yes sir…I will just copy these files to my iPad" Mr. Rajput replies. Professor Fabulous quickly goes to use the restroom. While Mr. Rajput is copying the files, he gets a call on his mobile phone

"Hello…" says Mr. Rajput

"Mr. Rajput…" replies a female voice

"Yes…" he says

"Mr. Rajput…Annapurna here, from Twitter India…" she says

"Oh yes…Miss. Annapurna…tell me and please hurry up" he says

"I am standing outside the gates of your headquarters; I had been to the Facebook office and got to know that Mr. Natarajan is here…" she says

"He is here… What's the matter" Mr. Rajput asks

"Can I come in… I think we have found a solution…" she replies

"What…" he asks with disbelief

"You heard me right … we have a solution…can you let me in…" she replies

"ok…" Mr. Rajput replies and instructs the security at the main gate to let Miss. Annapurna's car in by calling them on the intercom. After copying the files to his iPad, Mr. Rajput walks to the main entrance of the building. Miss. Annapurna is going through the security check. She is not alone. She is accompanied by two young men, dressed in black t-shirts having something written on it but is not clearly visible to read. Their laptops, mobile phones are taken away as per the standard protocol. As they pass the security checks and walk inside, Mr. Rajput reads the words written on their T-shirts which says "A Stupid Common Man" and below that, in smaller font sizes it says "Cybersecurity for the common man".

"Miss. Annapurna … you have to hurry… we are in a rush… and who are these two…" asks Mr. Rajput

"Sir…I am Sushant Agarwal…" one of them says before Miss. Annapurna could answer.

"And this is…" before he could complete, Professor Fabulous walks in from behind and says

"Rajput…Let us go…hurry up…"

Professor Fabulous looks at Miss. Annapurna and the two men dressed in black t-shirts and then looks at Mr. Rajput

"Sir…this is Miss. Annapurna, Twitter India head. She says they might have found a solution to recover from today's attack." Mr. Rajput says pointing at Miss. Annapurna

"And this is…" before he could complete Miss. Annapurna intervenes and says

"Professor Fabulous… Forensic Cyber Psychologist… I know…"

"Hello, Professor… how have you been…" she greets Professor

"Who are these two…" asks Professor Fabulous without bothering to reply to her greetings.

"Sir…I am Sushant Agarwal… and this is Abhishek Hegde," one of them introduces

"They have found a solution to stop this ransomware from spreading further and they can even clean the infected devices. It works for Twitter, but they are unable to test it on Facebook and WhatsApp until they get access to their source code, for which Mr. Natarajan is needed. And if it works, we will need the infrastructure of National Cyber Defense to deploy the solution" Miss. Annapurna says pointing at Sushant and Abhishek. Mr. Rajput recalls that in the meeting with Home Minister KRD this morning, Miss. Annapurna was very much focused on finding a solution for this crisis rather than tracking down the culprit.

"Another waste of time…Rajput we have to hurry…" says Professor Fabulous bluntly dismissing Miss. Annapurna

"Sir…at least hear them out…" says Mr. Rajput

"Rajputtttttttttttttttttt…" says Professor Fabulous in an irritated voice and reminds himself that Mr. Rajput doesn't trust him completely yet and he is trying to mend his broken relationship with him. Professor Fabulous takes a deep breath of patience and says

"Ok…I will wait for you Rajput… but hurry up…"

"You guys have ten minutes to explain to me, how are you going to fix this problem… if I am convinced, I will ask Magadi Sir to give you access to our infrastructure and Mr.Natarajan will come for free with it." Mr. Rajput says looking at Miss.

Annapurna, Sushant, and Abhishek.

"Sure Sir…" Sushant replies and he takes out a broacher and a visiting card and gives to Mr. Rajput and says

"Sir… we ran a small startup company called 'A Stupid Common Man'. We provide cybersecurity solutions for a common man such as password protection, online scam detection, data retrieval, personal information security…etcetera. This morning many of our clients, as a result of sharing fake messages on WhatsApp got infected by this ransomware and reported the issue to us"

Mr. Rajput is listening attentively while Professor Fabulous is not interested and is doing something on his phone. Officer Shirke also has joined in and is standing behind Mr. Rajput listening very carefully.

"Sir… you must also have run some diagnostics on infected devices…did you find a common pattern…" Sushant asks

"hm…Nothing…Costly and reputed brands like Samsung, iPhone, Nokia, Oppo and to cheap duplicate phones, Desktop and laptops operating on Windows or iMac or any other operating system, Cell phones with network providers like Airtel or Jio…everyone…everyone who was sharing false messages on Facebook, WhatsApp and Twitter were infected and that was only the common factor…" Officer Shirke replied, whose main job at National Cyber Defense is to run diagnostics.

"Sir… then you have missed the pattern…It is not the brand of mobile phone or the network provider or the OS of laptops." Sushant says and pauses for a moment and says looking at Mr. Rajput

"It is the microprocessor…which is common to all these mobile phones and laptops"

"What…did you say microprocessor," asks Mr. Shirke

"Yes…Sir… The microprocessor… all the infected mobile phones use ARM-based microprocessor and all the infected laptops use Intel-based Microprocessor…" replies Sushant

"Sir… have you heard of a term called Meltdown or Spectre…" he asks. Everyone including Mr. Shirke shakes their head left to right and right to left signaling no.

"Meltdown is a hardware vulnerability affecting Intel x86 microprocessors and ARM-based microprocessors. It allows a rogue process to read all memory, even when it is not authorized to do so. Meltdown breaks the most fundamental isolation between user applications and the operating system. This attack allows a program to access the memory and thus also the secrets of other programs and the operating system." Sushant explains and pauses for a few moments and continues

"In addition to Meltdown, we also found in our diagnostics that in some cases this ransomware was exploiting another hardware venerability called Spectre. Spectre breaks the isolation between different applications. It allows an attacker to trick error-free programs, which follow best practices, into leaking their secrets. In fact, the safety checks of said best practices increase the attack surface and may make applications more susceptible to Spectre" he pauses. His partner Abhishek Hegde who is quiet all this time continues from where Sushant had left and says

"Sir… and the most important point, this ransomware didn't infect the devices today. In fact, it has been residing on the devices for days or even months quietly collecting the data from everyone to study their Social Media behavior using these hardware vulnerabilities. After collecting enough data and refining the code using advance machine algorithms to detect false messages and fake news, the ransomware has only been activated today."

"Sir… knowing all these, what we have done…" before he could continue, Mr. Rajput intervenes

"Stop…stop…I understood" he says

"Shirke… take them inside and help them with whatever they need. I will talk to Magadi Sir, also tell Mr. Natarajan to give them access to Facebook" Mr. Rajput says looking at Mr. Shirke

"Ok Sir…" he replies

"Miss. Annapurna and you both… I think you are on the right track and I believe you understand the seriousness and urgency of the matter and hope that your solution works as you guys are expecting it to work before the devices start exploding…" Mr. Rajput reminds of the deadline set by ransomware of twelve hours out of which six hours have already passed.

"Miss. Annapurna…Shirke will help you with whatever you need. All the best…" Mr. Rajput says looking at Miss. Annapurna.

"Can we go now…Rajput…" asks Professor Fabulous who has been waiting for him patiently.

"Yes Sir…" he replies and they both hurry to a runway located five minutes away from headquarters of National Cyber Defense where a small military plane is ready to take them to Pune.

Chapter 10

The Ghost of the Past

Mr. Rajput and Professor Fabulous are seated in a small military plane and heading towards Pune. Usually, military planes are either fighter jets or large cargo style bombers, but this is a custom-made hybrid, with the size of a private jet and military-grade communication and security systems. Professor Fabulous is busy in digging more information from Google about the person of interest using Mr. Rajput's iPad. Even after 'clean slate' Professor is expecting to find something.

Every time he is searching the name of the person of interest, a patent filing is showing up. The title of the patent is 'Method and Apparatus of detecting deep fakes'. Upon reading the abstract of the patent Professor understands that it is a method of detecting fake videos posted on social media in real-time. He comes across various papers published by reputed engineering organizations like IEEE, WMC etcetera by the person of interest, related to the same topic of detecting false messages, fake videos, fake news in real-time on social media platforms.

While he is busy doing all this. Mr. Rajput is just staring at Professor with a little anger.

"What happened Rajput..." asks Professor Fabulous

"Why...why so much of arrogance... Professor... somebody is genuinely trying to help... but as usual, your arrogance blinds you to see beyond yourself" Mr. Rajput says referring to his blunt dismissal of Miss. Annapurna and the two boys. Professor keeps the iPad on the neighboring seat and says

"In psychology, there is a term called 'the arrogance of clarity'... do you know...what it is..." Professor asks

"No... I don't know...you are Psychologist not me..." Mr. Rajput replies

"It means, when a person is crystal clear in his mind about something or someone, he does not encourage any kind of discussion about it...but in doing so, the person is often perceived as arrogant. Like you are perceiving me" Professor says very calmly looking straight in the eyes of Mr. Rajput.

"But... how are you so clear in your mind... you are not a technical expert... you don't know a thing about software coding... you don't even know how to change the battery of your phone properly..." before Mr.Rajput could complete, Professor Fabulous says

"But yet, you sought my help, not any technical experts help... and you know very well why..."

"You know Rajput... why Sachin Tendulkar is called the God of Cricket..." asks Professor Fabulous to lighten the mood. But it is a rhetorical question and he answers

"It is not because of his centuries or highest runs or his boundaries or sixes. It is not because of his experience and precision of a technique in his batting or his simplicity and humility or his sportsmanship" Professor says in one breath and pauses for a few moments

"It is because of his one ability which no other batsman has… the ability to hit a sixer on the best ball, on the most difficult delivery of any bowler in the world. Hitting a sixer on a loose delivery … that anyone can do… but taking on the baller on his best delivery… that… only Sachin can do. That's why he is God of Cricket." Professor pauses and continues while Mr. Rajput is listening quietly

"And that's what this attack on social media is all about. This person is not targeting the weakness of social media…he is instead targeting the strength of social media. If weakness is attacked, it is very easy to fix…because half the work is already done by highlighting the weakness… the remaining half is to fix it… but if the core strength is attacked… then it is almost impossible to fix it" he explains looking at Mr.Rajput

"Professor…why do I get the impression that you are secretly happy about today's attack. That you wanted this to happen… as if you were waiting for this to happen…" asks Mr. Rajput. Professor Fabulous does not respond immediately but after a few minutes he replies

"Why… Why do you say that…Rajput…"?

"I can't help thinking about it… Professor…"

"You have emerged as a major critic of Social Media… especially in the last four years … you have published three books, multiple papers and given talks in various forums around the world … all of which are against Social Media. But… despite all that… it has made no difference to these social media companies…despite all your sincere efforts… no one cares… fake news gets circulated every second to billions of social media users…no one cares…" Mr.Rajput replies

"Rajput… are you suggesting that I am behind this cyber-attack… because I having been vocal about fake news and social media…because I want social media companies to be held accountable for spreading fake news…" Professor says immediately and pauses looking at Mr.Rajput without blinking his eyes

"Are you seriously suspecting that I have any part to play in today's cyber-attack on social media…" he asks again staring at Mr. Rajput but there is no reply from him.

Both are looking at each other but no one is speaking. Both can see in each other's eyes that the new walls of trust, which were beginning to form are now collapsing, both can hear only the plane's engine rumbling as if the engine blades are tearing apart the new bond of friendship which had begun this morning after four years of waiting. Sudden and unexpected turbulence in the plane breaks the eye contact between them diffusing the tension. After a few minutes of turbulence when the plane is stable Professor removes his seat belts and stands up and says

"Look…Rajput… you know very well… I cannot work like this… If you have trust issues, then I can walk out… but before that I want to tell you…" he pauses

"Yes…I am secretly happy … not because social media is been brought down. Because this is my only chance to make things right with you… What you want to hear from me… that I am sorry…I made a mistake…" he pauses, Mr. Rajput is still seated with his seat belt on and listening to Professor Fabulous carefully.

"Yes Of course… I am sorry… I must have listened to you… There goes by not a single day…when I don't regret my decision. You were right … I was wrong… I must have allowed you to shoot him…but that is past… let it go now… Rajput…let it go…" Professor says and keeps looking at Mr.Rajput for few moments then turns around and walks towards the cockpit to check how long it is going to take to reach Pune. He is now thinking of returning to Bangalore instead of continuing his quest with Mr. Rajput.

The words said by Professor Fabulous reminded Mr. Rajput of Janvi. She had joined Mr. Rajput's team while he was posted in Mumbai Cyber Crime Division. This was his last posting before he quit the police department and joined National Cyber Defense. Janvi had trained under Mr. Rajput during her probation. She was like a sister to him and trusted him above anyone.

He was assigned a case of online prostitution and extortion. It was a high-profile case where state ministers in power were lured to have a sexual encounter or affair. These sexual encounters were then recorded, and the ministers were blackmailed. Since state ministers in power were victims of this sex racket, Maharashtra State Home minister was himself directly looking into investigation and a very high level of secrecy was maintained and there were strict instructions that no one apart from assigned officers should know about the case.

The entire racket was getting executed online. The suspect would communicate only through text messages using mainly WhatsApp. He would use a new number every time, which would always be an international number either from Dubai or Nepal or Egypt making it very difficult to track. The extortion money was collected in Cryptocurrency.

Victim ministers were befriended by these girls using the same phone numbers used by cybercriminal on WhatsApp. They didn't exchange any pictures rather did a video chat directly. These ministers were even unable to give a correct description of the girl's face to the sketch artist. The face of the girls in the recorded video was blurred. Interrogation with high profile escorts, local pimps, known cybercriminals had yielded no results.

Mr. Rajput and his team were going nowhere with this case and had miserably failed even to come close to catching this cybercriminal and with every passing day without any result, the pressure kept mounting. Seeing no other option Mr. Rajput had reached out to Professor Fabulous for helping him in this high-profile case with his own risk without informing higher authorities.

After going through all the facts of the case Professor Fabulous had concluded that the only way to catch this criminal would be a bait trap method. As per the plan, an undercover lady officer will create a Facebook profile with attributes given by Professor Fabulous, making it easy for the suspect to approach the girl and ask her to be part of this racket. Janvi had volunteered to go undercover despite Mr. Rajput's concerns.

Within a few days they had narrowed down on a person of interest and he had invited Janvi to meet him in a five-star hotel. As per the plan, a few minutes after Janvi enters the room, police would storm in and nab the cybercriminal.

Everything was going as per plan but that day by the time Mr. Rajput and his team stormed in the room, the suspect had found out and was holding Janvi on a gunpoint. To make things worse, Professor Fabulous had discovered that the suspect was his research assistant.

Seeing that he was holding Janvi at gunpoint Mr. Rajput was about to shoot him but Professor Fabulous had objected and had urged that he will talk to the suspect to surrender. As Professor had started talking to suspect, Mr. Rajput was very worried and scared for Janvi but had trusted Professor Fabulous. But unfortunately, the suspect pulled the trigger killing Janvi and got killed himself in return police firing. To date, Mr. Rajput finds himself guilty for Janvi's death.

Mr. Rajput had to take a lot of heat from higher authorities for bringing in Professor Fabulous without their approval and death of Janvi under his supervision. He was asked to resign else he was to be suspended. The final straw broke between him and Professor Fabulous when he came to know that Professor was in touch with the suspect during the investigation of this case and had texted him just before Janvi entered the hotel room. Mr. Rajput has not forgiven himself or Professor Fabulous for Janvi's death.

Another sudden and unexpected turbulence shakes Mr. Rajput and disrupts his journey of an unpleasant past. He sees that Professor Fabulous is walking back to his seat when another violent shake throws him off his balance and he is about to fall to the floor banging his head but at the right time Mr.Rajput jumps off from his seat and grabs Professor Fabulous

"Professor…" he yells and keeps holding him for a few minutes until the turbulence is over.

"Professor…are you ok…" he asks as the plane stabilizes.

"Yes...yes... I am fine..." replies Professor but does not thank. He takes Rajput's hand off him and proceeds towards his seat. Mr. Rajput is still standing

"We will reach Pune in another twenty minutes said the Pilot... Then I will leave you alone..." says Professor.

"Why... Rajput... why you didn't care to ask me... if I had tipped off the suspect...We had worked together and known each other very well... at least once... for old time's sake... you should have heard my side of the story..." says Professor.

Mr. Rajput walks to his seat and gets seated facing Professor and says

"What is there to ask Professor...it was obvious from the evidence... that you texted him right before Janvi entered the room..." Mr. Rajput replies

"Yes...It is true...I texted him right before Janvi entered the room. But it is not true that I tipped him off" Professor Fabulous replies

"What do you mean Professor..." asks Mr. Rajput

"Look...Rajput... he was one of my research assistants at university...I barely knew him...I was in contact with him just like I was in contact with my other research assistants... I had no clue he was behind the sex racket..." Professor Fabulous pauses and continues his explanation

"That day... when we were at the hotel...he texted me that... he wanted to talk to me regarding some topics which he isn't clear about...and asked me If I was in Bangalore..." he pauses

"Rajput... I replied to his text only with one word...NO...

That's it… I didn't tell him I was in the hotel; I didn't tell him I was in Mumbai… and didn't tell him that the police were coming for him… and trust me… I came to know that he was behind this crime, only when I saw him in the hotel room…" he pauses looking at Mr. Rajput and continues

"He must have seen me from his hotel room window… and the moment I said… I was not in Bangalore…he must have come to know that this is the trap which is set by me along with the police…"

"That's the truth Rajput… I am sorry for Janvi…I equally feel guilty for her death…" he pauses for few moments and places his hand on Mr. Rajput's shoulder and says

"I don't want your forgiveness… I don't want you to trust me… but I want you… to forgive yourself…it was an unfortunate event for which no one is responsible…"

"Landing in fifteen minutes … fasten your seat belts…" announces the pilot as he prepares the flight for landing. Professor Fabulous and Mr. Rajput both fasten the seat belts. Both are quiet. Both are looking outside in the opposite windows and are not making eye contact.

As the plane comes to halt after landing, Professor Fabulous is ready to exit

"Rajput… when I got your call… this morning… I really started believing in second chances…but I was wrong…you take care…" he says and tries to open the door of the plane and struggles with it for a few minutes. Mr. Rajput gets up and says

"It is the other way…" he says and pushes the handle to the

opposite side which lifts the pressured plane door. Professor Fabulous sees a military personnel and a police constable already waiting with the car to receive them. Professor Fabulous gets down and starts walking away, Mr. Rajput gets down and says

"No…Professor…don't leave. We have never left any case unresolved…so why this…There was a time I referred you as my fire brigade… and myself as Jethalal…and I still do… that's the reason I called you today…"

Mr. Rajput is referring to characters from Professor Fabulous's favorite daily Indian comedy soap "Taarak Mehta Ka Ooltah Chashmah" where central character Jethalal calls his dearest friend Taarak Mehta as fire brigade who helps him in the most difficult circumstances every time.

"I will never be able to trust you again as I did before… but given the criticality and urgency of the situation… I have no choice but to believe you… you will have my word… our past will not disturb the present…" Mr. Rajput says with utter seriousness.

Professor does not reply immediately, but after a few minutes, he answers

"Fire brigade never leaves his friend Jethalal in deep waters and flees the boat…nor will I…orphan you in midst of this crisis… I know you have trust issues with me…but keep that away… until we nail this bastard…let's go now…we are already running out of time…"

Without wasting any time, they both get seated in the car and leave to the address mentioned in the passport.

Chapter 11

THE PERSON OF INTEREST

Sameer Pai is the person of interest that Professor Fabulous and Mr. Rajput have narrowed down. He completed his Engineering in Computer Science and had started working in a startup company before going to UC Berkeley. Sameer is the only son. His father is a retired assistant bank manager and his mother is a retired Marathi schoolteacher. During his Engineering, he had published many papers and studies on advanced machine learning algorithms which had bagged him a scholarship for studying Masters in UC Berkeley. Later at UC Berkeley, he focused all his effort on creating the software which can detect fake news on social media in real-time by use of advance machine learning algorithm and artificial intelligence. This was the same software which he had shown to Professor Fabulous at the conference.

Sameer's family is not rich, but they are very academic and culturally oriented family. His father hails from Honnavar, a small coastal town in Karnataka and had studied with the legendary Nag brothers who are famed for giving "Malgudi Days" to Indian television. He was a very active participant in Yakshagana, a traditional Indian theatre form developed in coastal and few other parts of Karnataka. His mother hails from Nipani, another small town in the border of Karnataka and Maharashtra which mainly speaks Marathi. His mother is a Marathi theater fan and enjoys watching any Marathi play. Having two culturally rich parents, Sameer was exposed to very liberal and open ideas right from his childhood. His concern for the rise of fake news and desire to curb fake news using technology was somewhere inspired by his deep-rooted cultural connection.

Professor Fabulous and Mr. Rajput reach Sameer's house. The two-storied house is surrounded by a small compound with the gate in the middle. The house itself is in the higher ground from where the entire Pune city is visible. There is a large cell phone tower located diagonally opposite to Sameer's house. The house is painted with distemper blue on the ground floor and the first floor that has only two rooms which are not painted. The two rooms have thick plastic sheet roofing instead of cement slab and have stairs from outside the house. These rooms look as if they were constructed for letting out for rent.

Professor Fabulous and Mr. Rajput both enter the compound and see that the main door is locked. Seeing them at Sameer's house, the lady standing in the next house says

"Hospital...gelee..." in Marathi, which means they have gone to the hospital.

"Sir... I will check in the neighborhood..." says Mr. Rajput and walks out of the compound. He takes the police constable along with him and starts asking in the neighborhood about Sameer and his family. Meanwhile Professor Fabulous goes to the first floor to see if anyone is there in the rooms. The rooms are not locked but only latched.

Professor enters one of the rooms which happens to be Sameer's room. The room is very neat and clean. The smell of lavender flavor room freshener is still in the air. The bed is neatly made with clean bedsheets and pillow covers. It appears it was cleaned an hour ago. On the right side of the room, there is a bookshelf that looks like the top view of a lotus flower having three rings. The outer ring with large sections, shaped like petals of a lotus flower, the middle ring having medium-sized sections shaped like smaller petals of a lotus flower. And the inner ring having a square and diamond-shaped small sections. At the center of this lotus flower formation, there is a digital photo frame that keeps displaying pictures of Sameer, his family, and friends, one by one like a PowerPoint slide show. There are few trophies kept below this digital photo frame. The three rings of this lotus flower-shaped bookshelf can be rotated. Any book kept in the bookshelf can be accessed by turning these rings.

"Very fancy..." says Professor Fabulous while rotating the outer ring of the bookshelf. He randomly grabs a book while the outer ring is still rotating. But what he has got is not a book. It looks like a photo album at first. But it is not a photo album either. It happens to be a collection of pencil sketches drawn by Sameer as a teenager. The sketches are drawn on a postcard and are autographed by personalities whose sketch is drawn on the postcard. On the bottom left corner of every card in very small font size, there is Sameer's signature which can be read clearly as 'Sampya'.

'Sampya' is Sameer's nickname given by his friends which stands for Sameer Pai. It is very common in Maharashtra and the Northern part of Karnataka to give these kinds of nicknames. Khanteesh becomes Khantya, Mahantesh becomes

Manthaya and so on.

As Professor Fabulous glances through the sketches he sees sketches of many famous personalities which include Late Prime Minister Atal Bihari Vajpayee, Late President APJ Abdul Kalam, Sachin Tendulkar, Anil Kumble, Rahul Dravid, Saurav Ganguly, Shahrukh Khan, Kajol, Anupam Kher, Ananth Nag, Nana Patekar, Bill Gates, Michael Jackson, Ben Kingsley, Pierce Boson and many others. Professor Fabulous guesses that there may be around two hundred to three hundred sketches.

At the end of this collection, there is the sketch of the famous playwright, writer, actor, director and theater personality Late Girish Karnad. After this sketch, there are no more sketches. Beside this autographed sketch there is a handwritten letter by Girish Karnad himself. The letter reads

"Dear Sameer

Your sketch reminds me of my teenage when I had a similar hobby of sketching portraits of famous personalities and sending it to them for an autograph. I had once sketched a great Irish dramatist Sean O'Casey and sent it to him for his autograph, but instead of a signed portrait, I received a piece of very valuable advice that changed the direction of my life. I am going to give you the same advice and hope it will also give a new direction to your life. Stop wasting your time with autograph collection rather than do something by yourself so that the whole world wants to collect your autograph"

The letter ends with Girish Karnad's signature and date.

"hm…Interesting…very interesting…Sameer took the advice very seriously and did something… by which the whole world will surely need his autograph… but it may not be in the same way people will know Sameer as they did Girish Karnad…" murmurs Professor Fabulous to himself and keeps the sketch collection back in the bookshelf.

Professor Fabulous sees few other books in the bookshelf kept in a separate section. The books are "Anti-Social" by Andrew Marathz, "The Cyber Effect" by Dr.Mary Aiken, "Anti-Social Media" by Siva Vaidyanathan, "Why Social Network makes us Unsocial", "The Civil War of Social Media" and many others including few books of Professor Fabulous, all of which talk about the way society has changed because of social media. While he is looking at these books, he suddenly sees a picture of Sameer and Mathew Maguire in the digital photo frame. The picture shows Sameer holding a beer in one hand and a barbeque stick in other, standing in front of a barbeque coal pit while Mathew is holding beer in one hand and barbequed chicken drumstick in other. After a few seconds, the next picture is displayed. This time there is a kid sitting on Sameer's shoulders who probably is Mathew's son and Mathew and his wife are posing holding their hands.

As the picture slide show continues, there are many pictures of Mathew and Sameer at the beach, at the party, at the bar, at the University all of them show that they both shared very good friendship. Seeing these pictures Professor Fabulous gets more confident that Sameer is the person who had called Manish Patel to avenge the death of Mathew Maguire and had hacked into his bank accounts. And Sameer is the person responsible for today's attack on social media.

Professor Fabulous sees a wooden computer table at the rear of the room. It's a small table with red and black sections. There is Apple's laptop on the table. The laptop has a red sticker of a camel-like animal that extends from top to the bottom of the laptop. The sticker looks familiar to Professor Fabulous, but he does not immediately recall. The table has some paper and a small notebook. There is a pen holder on the left corner of the table.

Professor Fabulous walks to the table and sits on the chair and starts the laptop. He is expecting the laptop to have a login password or even login by facial recognition but to his surprise, the laptop has no password. Professor Fabulous starts browsing through Sameer's laptop and finds various research papers, presentations, and other academic material. There is a folder that has only personal pictures and videos. He looks at few videos of Sameer having a good time with Mathew on the beach, few videos of his friends here in India, few videos of family gatherings. He is just seeing a few seconds of each video and closing them until he tumbles on one video which was shot in the same room.

The video shows Sameer standing in front of the lotus flower-shaped bookshelf and saying

"Hy…listen…listen…listen to this and tell me how it sounds…I am thinking of using these lines… in my talk…"

"ok… move a step back… and then say the lines…" a male voice who was recording the video says. Professor Fabulous stops the video and plays it once again.

"Hy…listen…listen…listen to this and tell me how it sounds…I am thinking of using these lines… in my talk…"

"ok… move a step back… and then say the lines…" the male voice says.

He stops the video again. And just plays the section of the male voice once again

"ok… move a step back… and then say the lines…" the male voice says.

"This voice… sounds very familiar…" Professor Fabulous murmurs to himself and continues to watch the video.

As instructed by the male voice Sameer takes a step back and starts saying the lines

"I am an environmentalist, but I am not against plastic…Yes… you heard me right… I am not against plastic… it will be highly impractical and unrealistic to think of life today without plastic. Somebody invented a marvelous material which cannot be destroyed for a thousand years… and can be used in ten thousand different applications including replacing and correcting a few of our body parts through plastic surgery. No, my friends' plastic is not our enemy … It is the monumental mismanagement of plastic which has led to environmental crisis…" Sameer pauses for few seconds and continues

"Similarly, I am not against social media, thinking of life today without social media is highly unrealistic. Somebody invented a way to connect everyone on this planet. But what I am against is this epidemic of fake news which social media companies are failing to address. And that's why I am here to offer a solution…" he pauses

"How is it…" Sameer asks taking a few steps forward

"hm… it is ok… but too long… make it short and crisp…"

replies the male voice recording the video.

"Try that climate change line...the one you had told me the other day..." he says

Sameer takes a step back and says

"Fake news is like climate change.... You can ignore it... but it will not ignore you... you can believe that it is not affecting you... but it is drastically changing you and the society you live in... every moment."

"Try that spiderman line...instead of climate change..." the male voice says

"With great power comes great responsibility, we have given these social media companies the power, now it is time to remind them of their responsibility..." Sameer says

"Ya... that is what I am talking about..." the male voice says. The video ends.

Professor Fabulous wants to see a few more videos but he is disturbed by a phone ring. It is a classic iPhone ringtone. He sees around the table, there is no phone. He gets up from the chair and starts looking for the phone in the room. The ring gets louder as he walks towards the bookshelf. He quickly searches a few sections of the bookshelf but does not find the phone. He then slowly starts rotating the outer ring of the bookshelf, the ring gets louder and louder. Professor sees a space grey iPhone in one of the sections as he keeps rotating the bookshelf. As soon as he grabs the phone the ring stops.

He takes out his phone and quickly dials the number found by Officer Shirke while running diagnostics on Sameer's identity. The phone rings again, this time displaying Professor's number. He is not surprised to see that it is the same number as tracked by officer Shirke, he was just double confirming that it is Sameer's phone. He disconnects the call after a few rings. The phone is locked by a four-digit passcode. Professor Fabulous just tries the default passcode which is one two three four and to his surprise, the phone unlocks.

He is about to browse Sameer's call records and text messages, but he hears Mr. Rajput looking for him

"Professor…Professor… where are you…"

"Sir…Sir… where are you…"

"Here…here…Rajput… on the first floor… in the room…" Professor replies

He can hear Mr. Rajput running up the stairs. Mr. Rajput enters the room pushing the door with a thud.

"Professor…Professor…Sameer…Sameer…" he says pausing to catch a breath

"Where…where is Sameer… did you find him…" asks Professor Fabulous.

"He is dead!!! Sameer is dead!!!" Mr. Rajput says with shock and disappointment. But the feeling of disappointment is not for Sameer's death but rather for losing the only hope he had to catch the culprit behind today's attack. He is feeling very dejected, hopeless and helpless.

"What!!! how is this possible…look at this room…neat and clean…as if it was cleaned an hour ago… look at this phone… this is Sameer's phone… somebody called on this number just a few minutes back… that means they were expecting Sameer to answer…." Professor says in complete disbelief

"He was murdered… about a year ago…

That's it…Professor… it is the dead end… all the information we have… is pointing to Sameer… but he is already dead…" he says looking at Professor. There is silence for a while as Mr. Rajput looks around the room helplessly and Professor is browsing Sameer's phone.

"No…No…Rajput…It is not over yet…there is never a dead-end of anything… its only lack of our ability to see other options and reach out to the truth…" Professor says after a few minutes.

"This is Sameer's laptop…take this… This is Sameer's phone…" he says pointing to laptop kept on the table and holding Sameer's phone in hand

"I have seen a few videos on Sameer's laptop. I believe he has a partner…" he says, which is only a guess as of now to give Mr. Rajput some hope that they have not lost the game yet.

"Professor…I know you are die-hard optimist… but… it is over… we don't have any other leads…" Mr. Rajput says

"Rajput… we are very close…very very close… don't give up on me… I am very sure Sameer had a partner…Please… trust me on this…" Professor makes a plea to Mr. Rajput, but he doesn't respond

"Rajput… you explained to me this morning about the 'clean slate' program… that somebody cleaned up all information about Sameer on the internet but failed to infiltrate government databases…" Professor says looking at Mr. Rajput

"Think about it for a second Rajput... If Sameer is dead... who else would benefit from deleting all his information... especially about his death..." Professor says

"Whoever is behind this attack... very well knew that we will focus on Sameer... and come hunting for him... in fact he wanted us to come looking for Sameer so that we waste our time on Sameer... while the actual mastermind stays out of focus..." Professor says trying to convince Mr.Rajput. While he does not look completely convinced, he is willing to give one more shot to find Sameer's partner listening to Professor's argument.

"What did neighbors tell you about Sameer's death..." Professor asks

"Nothing much Sir... only that Sameer was murdered about a year ago... and his mother has lost her mental balance after that. She believes that her son is still alive and is coming from the United States after two years. She spends her whole day cleaning and maintaining Sameer's room and his belongings. Sameer's father takes her to therapy every alternate day and probably that's where they have gone even today..." Mr. Rajput replies

"Hm... that explains why this room is so neat and clean. Absolutely spotless..." he says

"Anything else..." Professor asks

"There is some connection between WhatsApp and Facebook... to Sameer's murder... but the neighbors are not clear..." he replies

"Revenge...its revenge again... maybe there is someone...

maybe a friend who is trying to avenge Sameer's death by bringing down Social Media..." Professor says in a very affirmative voice.

"Where can we find more information on Sameer's murder..." he asks

"Sir... in the nearest police station... it is only a ten-minute drive from here...we must be able to find all the facts of the case there..." Mr. Rajput replies

"Let us go then..." Professor Fabulous says and both leave the room. They take Sameer's laptop and phone with them.

Chapter 12

LYNCHED AND MURDERED

While waiting for the sub-inspector in the police station Mr. Rajput is browsing Sameer's laptop and Professor Fabulous is busy with Sameer's phone. There are hundreds of photographs of Sameer with Mathew's son on his laptop.

"He was really crazy for the kid…" he says

"I am sure Sir… it is not because of Mathew's friendship Sameer took revenge on Manish Patel… it is because of this kid… just look at the immense love in Sameer's eyes for this kid… in every photograph…" Mr.Rajput says showing the photographs to Professor Fabulous.

"Sometimes I wonder… why most of us… fall madly in love with children…even the most arrogant person in this world who could have never said sorry even once in his life… even such a person will come to his knees… begging… if it is the matter of his children… even the most evil cruel and brutal criminals shed tears… when it comes to children…That's why they rightly say… God resides in children…" Mr.Rajput says

Professor sees that this is the first time Mr. Rajput has opened a little since morning and he is behaving like earlier when things were all good before Janvi's death.

"There is a very good psychological reason behind that Rajput…" replies Professor Fabulous

"And what is that Professor…" asks Mr. Rajput

"Do you remember what you did when you were nine-month-old or three-year-old or even for that matter until six-year-old…"

"Hm…my grandmother once told me that I had caught a scorpion in hand and was playing with it…" he replies

"But before your grandmother told you…did you remember that you caught scorpion…" asks Professor, Mr. Rajput shakes his head indicating no.

"you, me and almost everyone in the world will never remember what they did when they were very young. The brain just deletes that information. Somebody else like our parents or grandparents or elderly relatives should tell us about it… only then we know about those days, isn't it… Rajput…" asks Professor

"hm…I never thought about it… but I think you are right…" he replies

"As we grow up… we develop some sense of smartness and start understanding that every transaction in this world either emotional or practical, either personal or professional, is basically, give and take. Other's loss is my profit… Even though we consciously don't admit it, our brain has subconsciously decided that there is nothing called as true selfless love. Everyone needs something in return…" Professor explains and pauses for a moment and continues

"But when we encounter young children who are still unaware of the crookedness of the world... we are bombarded with nothing but pure, honest, selfless, innocent love... the feeling which our brain can't digest as it is against the logic. That's why people do anything for children... which in normal circumstances they could have never done..." Professor explains

"that's awesome Professor..." Mr. Rajput smiles

"Anyway...Rajput... don't you find this strange that Sameer, a UC Berkeley student with such impeccable academic record has his laptop without any password." asks Professor Fabulous getting up from the chair.

"It is the Cyber Cell...sir... not Sameer" replies Mr. Rajput

"What Cyber Cell..." he asks

"Sir...you see that cross mark at the bottom of the laptop..." Mr. Rajput replies.

Professor Fabulous lifts the laptop, he sees a small cross mark drawn with a red permanent marker.

"Yes... I see that...Rajput... what is that about..." he asks

"Sir...as you may know the laptop or phone collected as evidence is handed over to the cyber cell for searching any digital evidence. If these devices are password secured and if the person doesn't cooperate or is missing or dead, we use professional hackers to break through the devices. Such devices are usually marked..." Mr. Rajput explains.

"Oh... ok... no wonder that his phone also has the default passcode..." says Professor Fabulous

"Professor… why do you think Sameer had a partner…"

Before Professor could answer, Sub Inspector enters the room and says

"Arre… Rajput Sir…"

"Desai… what a surprise… I thought you were posted to Nasik…" replies Mr. Rajput shaking hands with Sub Inspector Desai.

"Meet… Professor Fabulous…" Mr. Rajput says pointing his hand towards Professor Fabulous and continues

"Professor… this is Ramakant Desai, we had worked together while I was in Mumbai…"

After exchanging greetings, Mr. Desai asks

"Tell me…Sir…what brings you here… from National Cyber Defense…"

"Sameer…Pai…" he replies

"We believe that he is…sorry… I mean… he was… behind this cyber-attack on social media. But after coming here we came to know that he is already dead… we wanted to find out more about his murder…" Mr. Rajput replies

"Hm… Sameer Pai murder case you don't know… it was all over the news when it happened about a year ago…" Mr. Desai says looking surprised. Both Mr. Rajput and Professor Fabulous shake their head indicating that they don't know. Mr. Desai instructs a police constable in Marathi to get Sameer's case file. All three of them get seated by the time constable gets the file and hands it over to Mr. Desai.

"Sameer was lynched and murdered because of this…" he says holding a photograph in his hand.

The photograph shows Sameer dressed in a black kurta and blue denim jeans, wearing a skull cap and a large metal cross pendant. He is holding a sword in one hand and a knife in the other hand. The picture also shows that he has placed one of his feet on a 'Shiv Ling'. It is a very provocative photograph and can easily trigger communal passion. Mr. Rajput takes the photograph from Mr. Desai's hand and after seeing it carefully he passes the photograph to Professor Fabulous.

"It is fake…" says Professor Fabulous holding the photograph

"That's absolutely correct Professor… it is a fake…" Mr. Desai confirms

"This is the original picture; it was taken during a college fest when Sameer was performing some play…" he says holding another photograph in his hand. The photograph shows Sameer in the same black kurta and blue denim jeans except that he is not wearing a skull cap or a cross pendant. The picture also shows that he is holding a sword in one hand and a knife on another hand expect that he is not placed his feet on a 'Shiv Ling' instead he has placed his feet on a chair.

The photograph was intentionally edited to spread communal hatred by conveniently adding skull cap and a cross pendant and replacing chair by a 'Shiv Ling'.

"The fake picture was circulated on social media…mainly on Facebook and WhatsApp," Mr. Desai says looking at Professor Fabulous and Mr. Rajput, while they both are listening very attentively. Mr. Desai passes a printout which shows the Facebook post along with the comment section.

The caption on the picture reads "Enough is Enough". The comment section was full of communal hatred and death threats

"He could have never dared to this in an Islamic country… when are we going to learn…" said one comment

"Kill…the motherfucker…" said another comment

"Burn him alive…" said one more comment

"We will not tolerate this anymore…kill the bastard…" said another comment

"This is our peaceful minority … cut him to pieces…" said one more comment and on and on.

While Mr. Rajput and Professor are going through printout, Mr. Desai says

"But…When this was bought to Sameer's attention, he had managed to get the posting removed from Facebook. The printout is of the snapshot which Sameer had taken to show us before posting was removed. But he was not able to stop it from going viral on WhatsApp…"

"And as you already know Rajput Sir… the WhatsApp mob… they never think… they never care… they just forward…"

"The WhatsApp mob… was already craving for Sameer's blood… he had already started getting death threats…" Mr. Desai pauses and continues

"In fact, Sameer and his Father both had come to this police station and filed a complaint about the death threats. Sameer was the one who had given this original picture to the police."

Mr. Desai shows the police complaint given by Sameer and his father.

"But… before we could anything… the very next day… four people, who came on two bikes wearing a helmet had gunned down Sameer. Twenty-six rounds were fired. Sameer was dead on the spot…the entire incident was captured on the CCTV footage of the grocery store located diagonally opposite to the spot where this happened." Mr. Desai says and pauses and allows the facts to sink in. There is an awkward silence. But this silence has feelings of disappointment, frustration, and anger which can be sensed by all three of them.

"Irony at its finest…" says Professor Fabulous breaking the silence

"A kid who wanted to find a solution to the problem of fake news on social media is killed because of a piece of fake news deliberately spread on social media. He rightly said… we can ignore fake news, but fake news will not ignore us…" his voice breaks as he speaks.

While Professor is emotional, Mr. Rajput is finding it hard and impossible to believe that Professor Fabulous didn't know anything about Sameer's murder. Professor had published many research papers and books in the last four years which are all based on the spread of fake news on social media. He has been very vocal in criticizing the social media companies for not doing enough to stop the spread of fake news. Professor has filed many petitions requesting the government to hold social media companies accountable for the spread of fake news. He is the leading expert on cybercrimes, he is very proactive to follow up on any lead he gets to make his case against fake news on social media. For such an academic,

Sameer's lynching and murder must be primary evidence to make his case more visible to the government against social media companies.

Mr. Rajput can't help of thinking, that Professor has not been completely honest with him. Even though he has no evidence, but his gut feeling has been telling him from this morning that somewhere or the other Professor Fabulous is linked to today's cyber-attack. He is very confused and is not only questioning his own decision to bring Professor Fabulous into this but to hold on to him even after Professor had offered to walk out. While all these thoughts are bothering his mind, Professor asks Mr. Desai

"Did you find out who had spread the fake picture…"

"No… we could not track the origin… but during a routine inquiry, many of Sameer's friends told us that, Sameer had a heated argument and a fight with Ramesh, who was his classmate in Engineering college during a re-union party just a few days before this incident happened. The argument started with Sameer objecting to Ramesh constantly forwarding political motivated fake messages of religious hatred in the college WhatsApp group. Most of his friends were of the strong opinion that Ramesh may have been behind this. Also, Sameer and Ramesh had a long history of rivalry during four years of Engineering college." Mr. Desai replies

"Did you enquire with Ramesh…" Mr. Rajput asks

"Yes… we did, he doesn't deny that he and Sameer didn't share a good relationship. He also agrees he had an argument and fight during the college reunion party. But he denies any wrongdoing. And there was no evidence against him." He replies

"What about the murderers…" Mr. Rajput asks

"We miserably failed to even come close to finding out who these murderers were until recently one of the accused in Gauri Lankesh murder case in Bangalore revealed that even Sameer's murder was done by the same gang along with murders of M M Kalburgi of Dharwad and Narendra Dabholkar of Pune," Mr.Desai replies.

"During your investigation, did you come across anyone, especially in friend circle, who was very angry instead of sad for Sameer's death…" Professor asks

"hm… Sameer was a very bright young man…he had a very good friend circle… everyone was very sad… I don't remember anyone being angry…" Mr. Desai replies

"Is there anything else Desai…we should know…" asks Mr. Rajput

"Officially there is nothing more to know…I told you all the facts on the record…" he replies and closes the files in front of him.

"But off the record…there was this rumor in Sameer's relative circle… that Sameer was about to marry an American lady who was a widow, elder to him in age and even had a child. But since it was not relevant to Sameer's murder, we didn't care much about it." Mr. Desai replies.

Professor Fabulous and Mr. Rajput both look at each other. They both instantly know that the widow Mr. Desai is referring to is late Mathew Maguire's wife. Before they could ask anything more Mr. Rajput gets a call from his boss BF Magadi.

"Sir…" says Mr. Rajput answering the call.

"ok…ok… right away sir… we will be there in thirty minutes…" he says and disconnects the call.

"Sir… Home Minister K R Dwarkanath wants to see all of us… he is already in Pune. Magadi Sir, Mr. Natarajan, and Miss. Annapurna, have already landed and will directly meet us in the Home Minister's office. We have to go now…" Mr. Rajput says looking at Professor Fabulous.

"Ok…" Professor replies without any resistance like before.

"Thank you, Desai… Thank you… I will call you later…" Mr. Rajput says collecting Sameer's laptop from Mr. Desai's table.

"My pleasure Sir… and all the best…" Mr. Desai replies.

Professor Fabulous and Mr. Rajput leave the police station and head to meet Home Minister K R Dwarkanath. Mr. Magadi has texted address to Mr. Rajput, which happens to be the residence of a local minister who belongs to the same political party as of KRD. As discussed in an emergency meeting this morning KRD has been getting hourly updates from Mr. Magadi and now, he must be expecting some results from them. It is at 6 pm. In another two hours, the first set of devices infected by ransomware will start getting destroyed and by 10 pm all the devices will be destroyed if they haven't found any solution.

The chaos and commotion have somewhat reduced, but people are still trying everything to get their devices working again. With Social Media services suspended, there is absolute digital silence. News channels are repeating the same news again and again. The home minister has called for a late-night press conference to give an update on the crisis. There is no official update from Facebook or Twitter after suspending the service.

All news channels are talking to various technology experts and asking their opinion on the crisis. Cryptocurrency and World Crypto Bank have become the highest searched words of the day. High profile celebrities, politicians and people who can afford to pay rupees one lakh have paid the money, but their devices are still not working. Some are worried about their personal information going public and even have destroyed their devices by themselves to save the confidential information getting out. Some are worried about losing their costly devices, for some whose entire income was based on spreading fake news are miserable. Everyone from top to bottom of the social media chain is rattled, but no one has any solution.

Chapter 13

BACK TO SQUARE ONE

Professor Fabulous and Mr. Rajput are heading to meet Home Minister KRD, both know that they don't have any concrete result, but they are hoping for the best. Professor Fabulous is busy browsing Sameer's iPhone while Mr. Rajput has closed Sameer's laptop and thinking something very deep, running his fingers on the red sticker attached to the laptop. Seeing him in deep thought Professor asks

"What is it Rajput… what are you thinking???"

"Sir… I was trying to remember something about this sticker… it has been bothering me from the time you showed me this laptop in Sameer's room…." He replies holding the laptop facing Professor so that he can see the sticker. It is the red sticker of a camel-like animal that extends from top to the bottom of the laptop, even Professor Fabulous felt it looked familiar when he had seen it in Sameer's room.

"Ya… it looks familiar to me also… but I am unable to recall…" says Professor.

"Sir… there is this guy… I forgot his name… he had published this video of American soldiers gunning down Iraqi civilians on his website. He had named the video as Collateral Murder. He went into an asylum in Ecuadorian Embassy in London in 2012 and stayed there for quite long until very recently he was arrested and dragged outside the embassy…" Mr. Rajput says

"Are you talking about WikiLeaks and Julian Assange…" Professor replies

"Yes…Yes…Julian Assange…that's the name…" he confirms

"There was one more person with him… some German guy… he always had this sticker, this… the same sticker on his laptop…do you remember sir…" he asks

"Daniel Domscheit-Berg…" Professor replies

"Yes…Yes… that guy…Daniel-whatever… had this sticker on his laptop…I clearly remember…" he says

"Daniel Domscheit-Berg who is also known as Daniel Schmidt was the spokesperson for WikiLeaks… he was also referred to as co-founder of WikiLeaks…he is a German technology activist…" Professor says while Mr.Rajput does a quick google search about him on his iPad. He finds a video of the Wikileaks press conference on YouTube from 2009. In the video, the sticker on Daniel Schmitt's laptop can be clearly seen. It is the same sticker as it is on Sameer's laptop.

"Sir… this sticker I am talking about… it is exactly the same sticker…" he says and passes the iPad to Professor.

"Sir… I was wondering why Sameer had this sticker on his laptop. Today's youth of Sameer's age have stickers of superheroes like Ironman or Batman… some have religious stickers like a sticker of OM or cross or 786 or any other symbols like a sticker of showing middle finger… but why did Sameer had this sticker…" he asks

"Rajput… these all are indirect references to a person's influences, earlier people had posters or books as a reference to their influences, with changing times it has come to stickers or symbols or even emoticons…" Professor explains

"But… I am not surprised by this sticker… don't go by Sameer's age… he was far mature in his thinking… anyway… what is your point…" Professor asks

"Sir… I am thinking if Sameer drew his influences from this Daniel-whatever and if you are very confident that Sameer had a partner… then isn't it obvious that this guy must be somewhat like Julian Assange…" he answers with a lot of confidence.

"You… have become quite smart in the last four years Rajput…" The professor replies complimenting Mr. Rajput and goes back to browsing Sameer's iPhone.

"If Sameer is this Daniel-whatever, then who can be Julian Assange behind this cyber-attack…" Mr. Rajput asks

Professor Fabulous holds Sameer's iPhone right to his face and says

"This guy… this guy is your Julian Assange…he is the one behind all this…"

Mr. Rajput takes Sameer's iPhone in his hand and sees a series of text messages. The text messages are dated about a year ago. The messages are part of chat between Sameer and the other person who is not in Sameer's contact list and therefore a number is appearing instead of a name in each of the messages sent by this person. The phone number starts with +354, making it obvious that it is not an Indian phone number. Mr. Rajput quickly looks up for +354 country code and finds out it is a number issued in Iceland.

He starts reading the text messages

Sameer:

Look... I told you ... I don't need your money... and I don't want to be a partner with you... I will find some other investors...

+3547626617212:

Think about it... Sameer... you cannot win the battle against fake news staying within the ethical and legal boundaries. Your technology and my hacking skills... it will be a potent combination.

Sameer:

What you are trying to do is not only unethical and illegal but also sheer madness. I don't wanna be part of it...

+3547626617212:

The world could have never understood the dangers of radicalization of Islam if Osama never existed or the evil of fascism if Hitler couldn't have existed... People only care if it affects them directly... these are deaf people... they will never listen to you... until there is an explosion

If I am ready to become that bad guy and take all the risk... what is your problem...

Don't you want to eliminate fake news from social media...

Sameer:

We have spoken about this in great lengths... I don't wanna waste my time again and I don't wanna be a partner with you anymore.

+3547626617212:

I am going to buy out your entire technology… just say the number… one million dollars… five million dollars or twenty-five million dollars… … just say it… whatever you want…

Sameer:

I don't wanna sell my technology to you.
Now you should stop texting me before I block you…

+3547626617212:

Sooner or later I will have your technology it is just a matter of time… and remember we both want to do the same thing but you wanna be Gandhi and I wanna be Bhagat Singh.

There are few more messages from the same number, but before he could read all the messages, they reach their destination. Mr. Rajput gives the phone back to Professor

"It is not Julian Assange… It is Bhagat Singh… we are looking for…Rajput…" says Professor while taking the phone.

Mr. Rajput does not react to Professor's comments. They both are escorted to the private meeting room in the house of the local minister. All of them who attended the emergency meeting in the morning are present in the room only Professor Fabulous and the two boys who Miss. Annapurna had bought to find the solution are the new entry. Some are standing and some are seated. There is the noise of indistinct chatter and murmur in the room. Everyone looks disappointed, dejected and angry. Home minister KRD is not in the room yet. Mr. Rajput and Professor Fabulous get seated beside BF Magadi. While everyone is waiting for KRD, Mr. Rajput gets busy talking with Mr. Magadi and Professor is going through all the text messages on Sameer's phone.

"Tinnnnn…" that is the sound of message notification on Sameer's phone and it is a bit louder than usual. There is a sudden silence in the room as everyone looks at Professor Fabulous at once. Professor looks back awkwardly holding the phone in his hand and after a second everyone goes back to their discussions and noise of indistinct chatter and murmur fills the room once again.

Professor Fabulous is surprised to see the new text message which has arrived just now, it is from the same phone number of Iceland, the message reads

+34576266617212:

Had you been alive today, I am sure you would not have approved of my actions. But you would have been happy to see that people are repenting and pledging not to spread fake news. Had I done this a year before, I couldn't have lost you. But at least now I have hope that no other Sameer must lose his life because of fake news.

After reading the message Professor thinks for a while. It is crystal clear to him that this is the person behind today's cyber-attack. There is no more doubt about it. He thinks of calling him and asking Mr. Rajput to trace the call while he is talking to him, but he also is very aware that there is a risk of losing him forever. He certainly will not be that foolish to not know how to fake a call by bouncing it to multiple locations and the moment he will know that authorities are getting closer, he will vanish.

Professor Fabulous thinks that rather than he calling the mastermind and risking losing him forever, he will make mastermind call him by pressing the emotional trigger points. Professor being a psychologist has mastery in doing this. He thinks calmly and tries to remember the facts he knows till now about the person behind this attack. He knows that he had the same intent as of Sameer to eliminate fake news. He had offered Sameer a large sum of money to buy his technology, which means he is rich or probably super-rich. It is obvious that he is a hacker, as he mentions his hacking skills to Sameer. He admires, cares and has a soft corner for Sameer or else he couldn't have messaged on his number even after knowing that he is dead and lastly the most important he considers himself as Bhagat Singh in this fight. He is a revolutionary in this battle against fake news.

"Bhagat Singh…that is the emotional trigger," Professor says in his mind and tries to recollect as much information he can remember about Bhagat Singh. He starts replying to the message, he types

"I am Sameer's friend. I know you are behind today's cyber-attack on social media. Sameer had told me that you want to be Bhagat Singh of this battle against fake news. I want to remind you that Bhagat Singh just didn't throw bombs in parliament and went in hiding. He proudly stood in the courtroom and exposed British oppression in India by making his motives clear. It is not by throwing bombs he came to prominence, it was by making his ideas public, by making his voice heard, by explaining his motive behind the attack he won the hearts of people and forced British to consider him seriously.

You have already thrown the bomb and now If you really want to win this battle against fake news, you must explain the motive behind today's attack, you must make your voice heard.

In the next few minutes, I will be with Home Minister K R Dwarkanath, Facebook India head Mr. Natarajan, Twitter India head Miss. Annapurna, National Cyber Defense Chief BF Magadi. You can call me on Sameer's number, I have made arrangements to put your call live on YouTube and every news channel in India will telecast your call.

Be the man you always wanted to be, do the right thing, be Bhagat Singh"

As soon as he hits the send button on Sameer's phone, the room suddenly goes silent. Professor Fabulous looks around and sees Home Minister KRD entering the room. He quickly takes out his phone and sends one more quick text to his YouTube freelance journalist friend

"Be ready... It will happen at any moment now... telecast it live on your YouTube channel, inform every news media outlet," Professor writes in his text.

Without wasting any time KRD standing in the middle of the room asks looking at Twitter India head

"Miss. Annapurna... what is the update... is the solution working..."

Miss. Annapurna looks at both the boys of 'Stupid Common Man' they shake their head indicating no.

"We need more time Sir...we are very close..." she replies

"Magadi... what about the email sent to Natarajan..." he asks looking at Mr. Magadi

"Sir... the email came from Manila, Philippines. We informed the Philippines Cyber Crime Authorities. They acted very quickly and nabbed a local cyber-criminal gang. Upon interrogation, they confessed to sending an email to Mr. Natarajan but... they are not responsible for today's attack..." he pauses and looks at Professor Fabulous and continues

"They are not even Anonymous ... they just were trying to take advantage of the situation and extort money by setting up fake Cryptocurrency Bank webpage so that it looks like they are really behind this attack..."

"Natarajan anything from your engineering team …" asks KRD looking at Mr. Natarajan

"Sir, we are working on it… we need more time…" he replies

"Rajput…what about your status…" KRD asks looking at Mr. Rajput

"Sir… we narrowed down on a person of interest here in Pune, but he is already dead… But Professor has found that he had a partner who may be behind this attack" he replies

"hm… maybe… or maybe not…" KRD says and takes a long breath and continues

"So…basically, we are back to square one, we are in the same status as we were in the morning…"

It is exactly 7 pm. In one more hour, the first set of devices infected by ransomware will be destroyed and all the data on these devices will be made public. There is dead silence in the room as no one dares to give any false hopes or excuses for today's failure. The silence is disturbed by the louder than usual classic iPhone ringtone coming from Sameer's iPhone.

Chapter 14

FREEDOM OF REACH

Everyone in the room looks at Professor Fabulous at once. He takes out the phone from his pocket and as expected, his plan to press the emotional trigger has worked, it was the call from the same number of Iceland.

"No... we are not back to square one..." he says looking at KRD holding the phone in his hand

"Here is the mastermind behind today's attack...shall I answer the call..." he asks everyone waving the phone around the room while the phone continues to ring. Everyone is shocked and surprised and starts murmuring among themselves and the noise of indistinct chatter takes over the room once again.

"Silence..." shouts Mr. Rajput

"Answer it, Professor... before the call gets disconnected...we are already short of time..." replies Mr. Magadi

"And put him on speaker..." adds KRD

Meanwhile, the freelance journalist is ready to stream the call live on his YouTube channel. No one in the room is aware but all the TV news channels are already flashing breaking news about the masterminds call and are ready to telecast it live through freelance journalist YouTube channel. Some news channels have already declared the culprit is caught and is giving his confession live. Some news channels are already giving credit to Prime Minister and Home Minister for resolving the crisis. But the truth behind today's cyberattack on social media is still a mystery and all the secrets are hidden in this call.

Back in the meeting hall, Professor keeps the phone on the table and answers the call and places the call on the speaker. The call goes live on YouTube Channel also starts getting telecasted on TV News Channel

"Hello…" says Professor Fabulous, but there is no immediate answer.

"Hello…" he says once again, a little louder this time but there is no immediate answer, but he can hear someone breathing and some noises as though the mic is getting adjusted.

"I am Professor Fabulous… Sameer's friend…" he says and waits for the answer.

"Your research on stopping fake news on social media is impressive. But fake news cannot be stopped by writing books, publishing papers, petitioning the government, giving TEDx Talks…" a male voice replies seriously.

"Are you behind today's cyber-attack on social media…" asks Mr. Rajput, there is no immediate answer but after few seconds of silence

"Yes…Yes…I am…" he replies

"Are you working alone… do you belong to Anonymous… or ISIS…" asks Mr. Magadi, but there is no answer

"Are you using Sameer's technology to detect fake news…" asks Mr. Rajput, but there is no answer

"What is your name…are you Hindu…Muslim…Christian… who are you…" asks Mr. Kulkarni out of nowhere. KRD looks at him angrily.

"Sorry…Sorry…Sir… was trying to find if, he is Desh Bhakt or Anti National…" Mr. Kulkarni apologizes to KRD.

"Vijay…Dinanath…Chohan… poora… naam…" the male voice replies quoting Amitabh Banchan's famous dialogue from movie Agneepath and giggling sarcastically and says

"I don't have time for stupid questions…"

KRD indicates to everyone in the room by showing the finger on lips to remain quiet and signals that only the Professor should talk.

"If my way of minimizing fake news on social media does not work…Then you tell me … how the fake news can be stopped…" asks Professor Fabulous

"You said… you are going to be with Mr. Natarajan, Facebook India head… why don't you ask him…" the male voice replies

Everyone looks at Mr. Natarajan expecting an answer

"a…ah…we can…a…we can…hm…we can…actually…" Mr. Natarajan struggles to answer

"Or perhaps Miss. Annapurna… Twitter India Head…" the male voice asks but Miss. Annapurna doesn't reply. There is silence for a few moments.

"You guys have no damn clue… isn't it… no damn clue… how

to deal with fake news…" he replies angrily

"Look mister… our job is not to stop fake news… we have strict community guidelines… if any post does not violate our policy we cannot take it down… even if it is false…we cannot take it down…it violates the fundamental rule of freedom of speech… and we are a company which is basically is made for freedom of speech…" Mr.Natarajan replies this time very confidently

"Hm…Freedom of Speech you say…Freedom of speech…" he says

"You know, when I started using social media, I truly believed that here is something which can replace the fourth pillar of democracy, here is something which can become the fifth estate and will be the shining beacon of enlightened democracy where people are empowered with truth and transparency. But I was wrong… in the name of freedom of speech social media has become nothing but a propaganda machine of fake news. The cancer of fake news is undermining the very foundation of democracy and you are giving lame excuses of freedom of speech…" he says very seriously. After a pause, he continues.

" I wonder Mr.Natarajan… had social media been around the pre-independence era… you could have allowed Bhagat Singh to be declared as a terrorist in the name of Freedom of Speech since such a claim will not violate your community guideline… and the same people who sing his praises today… could have forwarded tons of fake messages on WhatsApp and could have even lynched and murdered him on basis of this fake news." he says and pauses for a moment and continues

"Not only that… had you been around the Indian Freedom

movement … you could have convinced most of us that we are better off under British rule and there is no need for independence … and the same people who give the certificate of patriotism today … could have trended #BetterUnderBritish on twitter … using their twitter factory who do nothing but copy-paste from a series of tweets readily given to them…" he says very seriously.

Everyone in the room is listening attentively. Millions of people are hooked on to their TV listening to the call live, others having access to the internet are listening on YouTube live and have also started commenting on YouTube Channel.

"Who…are…you…" asks Mr. Natarajan

"Me…" he replies

"Yes…you… are you a hacker, political activist, journalist, cyber-terrorist… who are you…" Mr. Natarajan asks again

"Why… why do you ask… do you think only these people will have a motive to do this kind of attack Mr. Natarajan…" he replies

"I am the one who wants to wish his friend a happy birthday and Facebook bombards me with fake news to cure coronavirus by drinking cow urine, I am the one who wants to forward a tax document to his CA instead gets 130 fake messages about CAA and NRC on his WhatsApp, I am the one who wants to wish happy Diwali in his school WhatsApp group instead gets a fake picture of India at the night of Diwali by NASA… I am the one who wants to celebrate Holi peacefully instead gets bullied by #EcoFriendlyHoli… I am the one who gets Boycotted for standing with the students and I am the one who gets screwed for supporting the police … I am the one who sees a fake video and goes to protest the government and I am the one who sees another fake video and wants to burn all other communities... I am the one who becomes a Patriot by one tweet or Anti National by another tweet... and I am also the one who gets killed because of fake news which you refuse to take down because it does not violate your policy..." he says and pauses for a few minutes

"Yes, Mr. Natarajan... I am the one... whom you have taken for granted...pick anyone from two billion users of social media ... I am just an average social media user...who is fed up by your unwillingness to stop fake news..."

There is pin-drop silence in the room. Everyone is listening very carefully.

"You social media companies... have taken us for granted because we have allowed you to do so. Whenever someone shares, tweets or forwards a fake message instead of objecting to it, instead of holding the person accountable for spreading fake news, we keep sharing it, forwarding it, retweeting it or at the max, we will ignore." he says and pauses, everyone can hear him breathing through the speakerphone.

"But what can we do... we don't live in a vacuum... we live in a society... after all, we have to see the faces of the same people every day... even though the message is fake... no one wants to disturb their equation with their neighbors... friends.... and family... by holding them accountable for a piece of fake news and also, we are having other things to do in life ... to take care of family... to earn the bread... who has time to investigate the truth ... that's why we had mainstream media... that was the whole reason why media existed as the fourth pillar of democracy so that an average man like me...should not have to spend time investigating the truth so that trained, qualified experts with unbiased neutral voices can filter fake news from the truth and give us only the facts..." He says and pauses

"But mainstream media instead of verifying and debunking the fake news, they start behaving like lapdogs for their selfish gains…propagating and trending these fake news… presstitute bastards… There is not one media house which is not colored, everyone, everyone has their agenda…there is no neutral voice anymore… and when there is no neutral voice… there is no justice… no harmony…no peace… it is anarchy wearing the clothes of democracy … " He says and pauses

"My last hope was this government who had taken cyber security very seriously and spent Rs.400 crores…" he pauses and continues

"Why… Home Minister Sir… why are you not stopping the spread of fake news… why are you not holding fake news peddlers, social media companies accountable or for that matter social media users accountable for spreading fake news…" he asks and waits for an answer but no one replies.

"You don't care … you don't give a shit… about fake news … in fact you love it… because right now fake news is favoring you… it is giving you big political win…right now it is your most loyal friend… isn't it Home Minister Sir…" he says and pauses for few moments

"But… remember sir… most dangerous and hurtful betrayals do not come from enemies … they come from loyal friends… today fake news is with you… tomorrow it can be used against you… and it will be used against you… it is only a matter of time…" he says.

"Are you doing this because Sameer was lynched and murdered on basis of fake news..." asks Professor Fabulous

"Poor Sameer... bright young mind... not only with visionary ideas but also capable of turning ideas into reality... by the way... It was not Sameer who hacked Manish Patel... It was me and had Mr. Natarajan agreed to use his technology Sameer could have been alive...why don't you tell about that Mr. Natarajan..." he replies, everyone looks at Mr. Natarajan for an answer

"I don't remember the name... but there was someone from UC Berkeley who had approached us to demo his technology for detecting fake news in real-time...even though it was very impressive technology...we had reservations regarding usage of it... that is why it was rejected..." he replies with little hesitation.

"Tell them the truth Facebook India head..." he says very seriously, but Mr. Natarajan doesn't reply

"Tell them...that you are very much aware that ninety percent of social media users indulge in peddling fake news, this may be intentional or unintentional, this may be harmful or harmless, but they do it...

Tell them, that your business runs because of fake news.

Tell them, that your existence is because of fake news.

Tell them, that not only you feared Sameer's technology, but you tried to kill his technology by not allowing any other social media platform to use it..."

"Tell them Facebook India head... tell them...the truth..." he says, anger and frustration in his voice can be sensed by everyone.

Mr. Natarajan is getting cornered, he knows that if it goes on like this, more ugly truths will come out. He takes a firm stand

"I don't find it necessary to explain the business decisions to you… you are nothing but a rogue cybercriminal… we have done nothing illegal either here in India or any other country… If we were supporting fake news peddlers, why didn't the government stop us… and who has put you in charge… Home Minister K R Dwarkanath is here… ask him if we have done anything illegal…" Mr. Natarajan says, cleverly passing the monkey on his back to home minister KRD.

There is no reply from the other side of the phone. After waiting for a few seconds, Mr. Natarajan says

"Quit… quit the social media if you have so much problem with it … no one is stopping you… many have done it and living peaceful happy life… quit the social media… and stop this nonsense"

There is no immediate reply, but everyone is waiting for the answer, the man coughs and says

 "I am not against technology…I have always considered social media as the greatest invention of the 21st century and I am not doing this for Sameer or anyone… I am doing this for myself… I want every social media user to enjoy his time on a platform without getting bog down by fake news… I don't want my children to graduate from WhatsApp University. I don't want our elections getting hacked by fake news, I don't want to get a cure for HIV by becoming vegetarian… this should stop, this is not acceptable…"

"Then what the fuck do you need…" shouts KRD

"Patience… Home Minister Sir… Patience… right now I need your Patience…" he replies

"Damn it…" KRD yells in frustration

"Do you know how many petitions have been filed by Professor Fabulous and other academic scholars, backed with well-documented research showing the ill effects of fake news on society and the way democracy is getting undermined. They have been requesting to take action against social media companies and individuals for spreading fake news… do you at least know… Home Minister Sir…" he asks

"No… I don't know… and I don't need to know… because there is already a law for it… there is already a legal procedure for it… if you find any social media content derogatory, the doors of the court are open… go to any police station and file a complaint and strict action will be taken…" KRD replies

"And what is that strict action… Sir…" he asks, there is no reply from KRD

There is silence in the room. Home minister KRD is a seasoned politician, he knows very well that this is no time for argument. For one argument, the person behind this attack can give ten counterarguments. He quickly changes his strategy and calms down and tries to pacify him by saying

"You are right…I admit… There is an unwillingness from both, social media companies and the government to curb fake news. I acknowledge that we are not doing anything to stop fake news…we are wrong … but that does not make you right… that does not justify your actions, this is nothing less than a terrorist attack…" he waits for a few seconds, but there is no reply.

"If you don't want money… what do you want… do you want the Government to punish your friend's murderers … what is his name…" KRD pauses to remember the name

"Sameer…Sameer…Sir…" one of his advisors in the room whispers

"Ya… Sameer…your friend…do you want us to hang the culprits…" asks KRD.

"You should do that anyway Home Minister Sir… isn't that your job…this… this… is the state of your governance … that if somebody wants justice, they should threaten you… isn't getting justice our basic right… given by our constitution… Sir…" he replies

"Look… this is not a time to debate on freedom of speech or constitutional rights… tell us what you want…and end this…" asks Mr. Rajput

"Since Sameer's death has been bought up… I want to ask you… who do you think murdered Sameer…" he asks, everyone in the room looks at each other.

"Some criminals who fired twenty-six rounds on him…" replies Mr. Rajput

"ah… *Afsoos ye gallath jawab*…" he replies sarcastically imitating famous lines of Amitabh Banchan from TV show Kaun Banega Crorepati.

"The creator of the fake picture…" Mr. Rajput replies again…

"No…No…Rajput… it is not the criminals who brutally gunned him down… it is not the creator of the fake picture… it is the people who forwarded these WhatsApp messages without caring to know if it is true or false…" replies Professor Fabulous

"Bingo… Professor… It is these people … these people who have given up reasoning… questioning…thinking… I want to punish these people… In the entire world, Indians are known for asking questions… even in the United Nations, you will see only Indians asking questions… but when it comes to social media… just forward, share or tweet… don't care to know the truth… " he says and pauses for few moments

 "With every fake message forwarded or tweeted or shared, these fake news peddlers are making a statement and asking a question… that we are going to fool you like this every day… every minute… We are going to fool you during elections, We are going to fool you about government policies, We are going to fool you about religion, We are going to fool you about war, We are going to fool you about the economy, We are going to fool you about nationalism, We are going to fool you about vegetarianism, We are going to fool you about corona virus, We are fooling you about reducing weight, We are going to fool you about the new currency, We are going to fool you on Diwali…Holi…Independence   Day…Eid…Christmas…New year…We are going to lie and fool you about every damn thing on this earth … and you cannot do anything about it…" he pauses for a moment

"yes… this is the question every fake news peddler had asked me till now and I am answering all of them today. No motherfucker can forward me a fake piece of shit and fool me… I am not going to tolerate this anymore…" he pauses and coughs

"And the most disgraceful...disgusting... and the painful thing is to see... that these people are giving away the most incredible thing given to us... only to us Indians... for the sake of forwarding or sharing or tweeting a fake piece of information..." his voice breaks as he speaks

"And what is that one thing only we have which others don't..." asks Professor

"I am a well-read, well-traveled man... Professor... In my entire life, I have seen, either here in India or outside India... whenever we are given the right opportunity... whenever our talents are recognized... we have excelled at the speed of light... just list CEO's of top ten companies today... we will surely find more than half of them will be of Indian origin... you pick whatever sector... given a fair chance... we have excelled..." he pauses for a few moments and continues

"This is not magic... this is not luck... it is because of one precious thing... called cultural genetic intelligence...which has been passed on to us... from generations to generations from five thousand years..." he says. Everyone is listening very attentively, including people who are hooked on to their television sets. He continues after a few seconds

"You go to any remote village... in India... talk to any person... he may be poor... he may be illiterate... he may be having lesser knowledge... he may not know how to use technology... but... he is not a FOOL... he will have greater common sense and IQ... and all these people who are infected by my ransomware are giving up that precious gift of common sense and getting fooled. I can accept people being evil rather than tolerating a fool… and I will not let this happen…" he says. There is silence, no one is talking. KRD once again refocuses on the current crisis

"What do you want… do you want to hang them… for forwarding a false message…" he asks

"No…No… KRD sir… I don't want these people to be hanged. Your government is passing revolutionary bills these days in parliament… just pass one more bill… 'Fake News Bill'…" he says and pauses for a moment.

"I don't want any criminal punishment … I don't want any jail time in this bill… the problem of fake news is created by technology…so the punishment should also be related to technology… That's why… I want three simple things on this bill

First, end the anonymity on social media. If we can link our AADHAR card to our mobile numbers, then for sure we can link our Facebook account, our Twitter account, our WhatsApp or any other social media account to AADHAR. This itself will cut the fake news by half.

Second, cut the lifeline…and I am not talking about cutting power supply or water supply. The lifeline of today's world is the mobile phone and the Internet. Everything is linked to our mobile number today, our banking is on phone, our shopping is on phone, our taxi is on phone, our romance is on phone, our LPG is on phone and even our food is on our phone. Punish by blocking the phone number, which was used to propagate fake news and prohibit from obtaining a new number.

Third, make disclosure of social media history mandatory for any job, private or government it should be mandatory. And if a person is found to be sharing fake news, disqualify his eligibility to apply for a job…"

"Will you pass this bill KRD sir… I will terminate this cyber-attack right now…" he asks after explaining what he needs in Fake news bill. There is no answer from anyone. After a few seconds of silence

"Even If I agree to pass this kind of bill…how and who is going to decide what is fake news and what is not…" asks KRD

"hm… now you are asking something useful. Professor Fabulous, can you explain to everyone the ways of detecting fake news… as you had proposed in one of your books…" he asks Professor Fabulous

"Well… There are multiple methods. But fundamentally it boils down to two factors. Either identifying fake news after it is gone viral or detecting and filtering it before it reaches people. For identifying fake news after it has been posted on the social media platform, I had proposed that all social media platforms should have a 'verify' button which is backed by Advance Machine Learning algorithms which can do a real-time fact-checking…" Professor replies and pauses for a moment, but before he could speak further, Mr.Natarajan interrupts

"What rubbish Professor… do you even know how much computing power will be needed to verify the contents of billions of users; it is completely unrealistic, impractical and non-viable solution…"

"Look, mister … whoever you are…" Mr. Natarajan says and pauses for a second

"Problem is not technology… problem is this rubbish idea of

yours… you want to punish people for believing in something which is not true. For having the views which don't resonate with your views. And who are you to decide what people should believe in… If I believe in something which is not true… it is my wish… it is my freedom of speech…even if it is false… it is my freedom of speech… and that is a basic human value which everyone has … no one can be punished for that…" Mr.Natarajan is irritated.

"Oh shut up…Mr. Natarajan… you and likes of you… are having a serious misunderstanding that you guys are in the business of Freedom of Speech. You guys don't seem to realize that you are not in the business of Freedom of speech, you guys are in the business of Freedom of Reach. I can believe whatever I want to believe… like this stupid message which makes rounds on social media on every valentine's day, that Bhagat Singh was Martyred on 14th February, not on 23rd March or cancer can be cured by eating *sitafal*… or the earth is flat… and the other ten thousand false things… I can believe whatever shit… but the moment you give voice to my stupid believes to reach to millions of people…without vetting… that's the root cause of this problem. Freedom of reach… not Freedom of speech." he replies with anger. There is silence again, no one is speaking. He takes a few moments to calm himself down and asks

"Anyway… tell me KRD sir… will you pass Fake News Bill… Tell me Mr. Natarajan will you adopt technology that can filter fake news before it reaches millions… I will terminate my attack right now… or even come forward and surrender myself…"

Everyone in the room looks at each other. But no one answers.

"Your silence… is enough to justify my actions today…" he says after getting no reply from anyone.

"Do you think … you will never be caught… do you think you have killed social media by your ransomware…sooner or later we will find the solution to subvert your code…" asks Miss. Annapurna who has been quiet from the time she entered the meeting hall.

"No…No… I am not overconfident… I am realistic… I am very aware that with all your engineering force and money you will find a solution. I am very aware that the National Cyber Defense is tracing my call right now…" he replies. Professor Fabulous looks at Mr. Rajput who nods and confirms that the call is getting traced.

"I am very well aware that I can be caught and killed… but I have done one thing very important today…" he says

"I have held people accountable for spreading fake news… In the future, they will think twice before sharing any messages. Through this attack, I have made a loud statement to the deaf social media companies and government that, fake news will not be tolerated anymore. There will be serious consequences. You can't hide behind freedom of speech anymore. I will not allow you to fool us…anymore…" he says and pauses

Meanwhile, Mr. Murthy, KRD's secretary comes running in the meeting hall opening the door with a thud.

"Sir…Sir… the call is live on TV… everyone is hearing the call live on the TV…" he screams

"What…how… stop the telecast… right now…" yells KRD. The room is filled with indistinct chatter and noise of shock and surprise.

"Professor… disconnect the call…" Mr. Natarajan yells

"Yes… disconnect the call…" yells IT minister

"Professor how can you do this… how can you do this without telling me…" asks Mr. Rajput

"Just like you put the call on the trace without telling me…" replies Professor

"Professor … disconnect the call I said…" yells Mr. Natarajan once again. Everyone is going crazy and yelling, no one can hear anything. Mr. Murthy comes running to disconnect the call.

"STOP…………………." shouts Professor

"STOP……" he says again

"There is no need to disconnect the call… he is already gone." He says holding the phone in his hand. The call had already got disconnected by the time Mr. Murthy entered the room.

Chapter 15

THE AFTERMATH

Twelve hours have passed. The first set of devices start getting destroyed. The screen of the devices flickers heavily before accepting death with a sharp blip on the screen. Devices of the people who paid money are not destroyed, but all the data on the devices including the contact list is wiped out. No data is made public.

At the same time on the other side of the globe in the United States, the stocks of social media companies came crashing down pulling down the overall global share markets. The blame game has already started in India, government blaming social media companies, social media companies blaming phone and computer companies, Phone and computer companies blaming users for not updating the software, on and on.

The phone call trace was not successful. The call kept bouncing from Iceland, Malaysia, Dubai, Singapore, and many other countries. Mr. Rajput strongly believes that the caller was just a pawn in this game the real conspirator is Professor Fabulous. He doesn't know if he will be able to trust him ever.

Social media companies worry about the spread of ransomware to other countries. People across the globe are thinking twice before sharing anything on social media. Some of them have even quit social media altogether. Social media companies are struggling to find a solution but guided by the two boys of 'Stupid Common Man', they are on the right track.

Today's cyber-attack on Social media has ignited a raging debate across the world, across all the nations to take the issue of fake news seriously. Some nations have already started thinking about the 'Fake News Bill' as it was proposed by the attacker. Singapore has already made a press release announcing that it will make changes to its existing law against fake news. Many other countries are already considering acting against fake news and forcing social media companies to adopt new technologies. Few companies have already started the process of buying rights to Sameer's patent on detecting fake news. But only time will tell if anything will change in India.

www.ingramcontent.com/pod-product-compliance
Lightning Source LLC
LaVergne TN
LVHW042108190726
843493LV00006B/1400